Micka and Me:
Ouroboros
By
Deborah. C.Foulkes

Sue
Many thanks

Deborah.C.Foulkes

Deborah C Foulkes

Copyright 2014 Deborah.C. Foulkes

This book is dedicated to my dad, who has always believed.

Deborah.C.Foulkes

Acknowledgements

I am very lucky to have so many good people around me that do nothing but show support. I'd like to thank Astrid for being there for me during the ups and downs as well as allowing me to take your name for my character. I'd also like to thank Simon for giving me a push when I hit a brick wall with this one. Your time and wacky wisdom means a lot. I would also like to thanks Sammy Bredesen for loving these characters and for giving me ideas and reading proofs. Also I would like to thank the anonymous contributor of the subtitle. I have no idea who you are, but it was perfect. My final thanks goes to Shannon for being the prefect daughter and not giving me any reason to worry. I love you.

The Story So Far…

Mina Marley lives in a town where supernatural beings try and live as humans. Her father, a fallen angel helps those who want to leave their magical realm to integrate within human society unnoticed. But when an angel called Micka arrives in town everything in Mina's world changes. She finds out that a group of renegade supernaturals called the Emandato want her dead, because their angelic leader believes she should never have been born.

There is also the time of the Cycle Glorious where all supernatural beings powers are heightened and it's fabled that something great will happen at this time for the human world. But the Emandato find her and attempt to kill her. Micka saves her and she finds out that she has five angel godparents to protect her, Micka included.

After being saved, Mina finally gets to tell Micka how she feels about him, but when the fabled Lord of the Manor, Sebastian Daniels arrives in town and the game changes once more. Micka disappears without a word leaving Mina heartbroken and with Sebastian helping pick up the pieces she finds herself falling for him too. But the Emandato have other plans and using another angel disguised as Micka, they lull her into false sense of security and make an attempt on her life once more.

The Cycle is over and Mina finds out the true nature of the Marley family. She's always known that she's half angel, but to find her mother was a succubus means that inside her is the power of the most powerful realms in the world. Confused, she runs off with Micka after finding out that Sebastian had him imprisoned. But while playing happy families, Mina's twenty seventh birthday approaches and she realises that to be a Marley she must endure the powers of heaven and hell and make the choice between the man she loves and the man the Powers that Be what her to be with.

Post Dragon

Mina's Online Blog 24th April 2200hrs

'Where is she? You can't stop me from seeing her.'

'You're right. That's always been the problem I've never been able to. But you must know now that she's gone through her own choice.'

The raised voice of Micka and the calm one of Sebastian wakes me from my deep slumber. Bleary-eyed, I try and focus on where I am. The bed is huge and I mean huge, and elaborate. It's a four poster with carved wooden posts and a green velvet canopy. This must be Sebastian's bed. I don't even remember getting here, but then the previous night is like a blur.

I've no time to think about it too much before Micka's voice causes me to stumble from beneath the covers. Every part of me aches after the night with Sebastian. I feel like I've been pulled through the wringer and not quite made it to the other side. The whole day and night had been one I never wanted to experience again and the hangover isn't pleasant ether.

Grabbing the first thing on the floor, which happens to be Sebastian's shirt, I've no choice but to pull it on. I get to the top of the stairs and taking a deep breath, I prepare to face the man I've betrayed.

'Clegg, would you mind seeing if Miss Marley is awake. You'll find her in my room.'

I flinch, feeling the impact those words will be having. Sebastian is not taking any prisoners, but who can blame him. Micka has always won, but not this time. This time I came crashing down and brought Micka with me, burning him on the way. Taking one more deep breath, I step round the corner and make my way down.

'I'm here,' I say.

Jesus Christ what have I done?

I've never seen Micka in such a state before. Dishevelled clothes and none of the calm stillness he's always possessed. His eyes are tormented as they catch mine. Sebastian comes to my side and rests a hand on my hip, causing me to swallow down all feelings that start to emerge.

'You don't have to explain yourself,' Sebastian says softly.

'It's okay. He deserves it,' I answer.

'Take him to the parlour then.'

Sebastian tugs me towards him and kisses me softly on the lips. Pulling away, I offer a smile before descending down the rest of the stairway. Silently, Micka follows me and I close us into the room. The smell of him still intoxicates me and my body responds, but it can't and mustn't happen. I must keep the redheaded angel's words to the forefront of my mind.

'Why are you here?'

Micka looks at me flabbergasted and it takes a moment before he answers. I feel heartless, but I have to do this.

'Uzrel told you to wait. Why didn't you wait?'

I don't answer and he takes a step forward causing me to take a step back, finding I'm near the wall as he follows. Hemmed in and cornered. Exactly how I feel.

'Mina, please tell me you've not…that you and he…?

I give him a slow nod. A deep growl leaves his mouth and I flinch as he punches the wall behind me. My heart stops for a moment, because I don't know how angry he really is. Deep down I know he'd never hurt me, but things have changed so much between us. Then he falls at my feet and starts to sob.

'I gave myself to you. I have never done that before. Does that not mean anything?'

I try and control every part of my body so it's stone still. The angel on the floor at my knees is nothing. He's in the way of what I need to have.

'I'm a Marley. What did you expect? It's what we do. We take what we can and then throw it away.'

'Please come back. We'll move on from this. I need you. I love you.'

'I'm where I'm supposed to be,' I say.

'I'll give you everything you want. Anything. Children. I want you to have my children. Let me be a father. The wings are no longer important just come back to me.'

'It's over! I want nothing more from you.'

Micka lifts his wet face. I really have broken him. I've taken a reputedly strong militant angel and smashed him to pieces. I should never have let it get this far. I should have stopped it. I most certainly should never have slept with him. But it was all about my feelings and what I wanted. Now it's down to me to clean up the aftermath.

'You said you loved me,' he says.

'Micka, you are my godfather, just like Uz. Maybe it's time you went back home. I don't need you anymore.'

I push past him toward the door and pull it open. Micka stumbles to his feet and stands stock still. Then he turns towards me and there he is. The angel that I first met—eyes cold and distant. With his shoulders held back, he moves towards me and stops.

'Your father gave you a book,' he says coldly. 'I suggest you read it again. That way you'll know what you've been sold to.'

And with that he storms out. He's gone. He's really gone. Panic fills me. Can I really let him go just like that? And why are my insides starting to chill and freeze. I'm changing and I'm not sure I like it.

What did he mean? Read the book again. Why? I already read it once. It's just a last word thing. Angels and their last words.

Sebastian slowly enters the room and looks at me worriedly. He's put up with so much from me and yet here I am. Our night together was different than ever expected. He was gentle and passionate allowing me to set the pace, while he followed. It felt as though months of turmoil and grief was at last appeased. I was sated and satisfied.

How could I have doubted that he was made for me?

Now in the doorway, he seems vulnerable. I realise then, that it's I that holds the power, because they all need something from me.

'Can I come in?' he asks.

'It's your home,' I say, sighing.

Sebastian wraps his arms around me and holds me a close. I turn to his heat. The cotton shirt he wears feels soft against my cheek and I close my eyes.

'I'm sorry,' he says into my hair.

'Why are you sorry?'

'Because it was I that told Ray to bring Micka to you. I wanted you safe. I just never expected...you know.'

I'm drained of everything and no longer feel anger. At the end of the day, the choices were my own. I chose to act on my feelings that others clearly told me not to.

'What plans do you have today?' I ask.

He looks down with his dark brown eyes and feel my body responding.

'Nothing that can't be put on hold, why?'

Taking his hand, I lead him out towards the staircase where Clegg suddenly appears.

'Clegg, could you serve breakfast to our room in an hour?'

I note Sebastian's raised eyebrows and a look of amusement of Clegg's face.

'As you wish, Miss. Marley.'

He disappears and Sebastian looks up at me.

'Our room?'

'Yes, our room,' I answer pulling on his hand.

'You've seem to have caught on how to speak to the staff pretty quickly,' he chuckles as we climb.

I stop and turn towards him as we reach the bedroom.

'Was it too much?' I ask.

'He's been waiting a long time for you to place that order,' Sebastian smirks, closing the door.

'Are we going to address the elephant?' Sebastian asks as we sit and munch through buttered toast.

'Why where is he?' I joke.

Sebastian gives me a look and I groan.

'Do we have to?'

'Yes, I think we do?' he says. 'You left me at our engagement party and spent near on two weeks with another man only to turn up on my doorstep barely dressed and in the rain. Not that I'm complaining about the outcome.'

'What do you want me to say? I made a mistake and I suppose it took me to do something stupid to realise it.'

Sebastian looks at me for a beat. His eyes searching mine. I know why. I've deceived him many times, why should he believe me now?

'So Micka was a mistake,' he says. 'A mistake you don't wish to repeat.'

'Yes, I'm here now with you. In the end, Micka was never enough. He just wasn't you.'

Relief floods his face and I still my lying heart. He smiles, then reaching over, kisses me. I scramble onto his lap, knocking plates and cutlery onto the floor. As our tongues meet, I press down against his hardness and start to grind my hips. He moans in my mouth as his hands move under the shirt to my naked breasts. His mouth travels down my neck and I lean back to give him easy access. We are both pulsating with need and again that serpent is stirring inside me.

'God! I'm not sure I can keep up with a Marley anymore,' he mutters.

What? Did I just hear right? What does that mean?

I pull away and the widening of his eyes tells me I've heard correctly.

'Sir!'

A knock on the door breaks the mounting tension as we both look at each other.

'What?' Sebastian growls.

I shuffle off his lap and start to gather the wreckage of breakfast so that I don't have to look at him.

Who is the other Marley that he had?

'You have guests,' Clegg says through the door.

'Like who?' Sebastian gets to his feet, making his way towards me.

'Mr. Marley times two and the angel.'

My father, Danny and Uz are here. What on earth is going on? Surely now I should be left alone. I'm doing what they all want. I can see Sebastian is desperate to stay and talk, but torn. He grabs his shirt and pulls it on before straightening his trousers.

'I asked Clegg to bring you some clothes. Join us when you're ready,' he says kissing my cheek.

I wait until alone and then start to wash and dress. I need to be quick if I want answers and I don't fancy seeing everyone when I'm half-dressed and still ruffled. Sebastian has a lot to answer for and I hope to god that the Marley was not my mother, because that is one thing I can't get my head round. My father and mother were first loves. That's what Ray said. Shaking my head clear, I make my way out and down the stairs.

I find them all huddled together in the living room. But there is no Uz. Instead, sitting in an armchair with steeple fingers on his chin and a self-satisfied look in his eyes is the redheaded angel. They all turn to look at me and I launch myself into my father's arms and hold him tight. This is what I need. I need my father after everything.

'I'm so sorry,' I whisper.

'Don't be,' he says.

'Are you okay?' Danny asks placing a hand on my back.

It's as though the three of them are shielding me from the angel in the chair. Who the hell is he that has made them all protective?

'I've had better,' I answer. 'Being a Marley is certainly painful. The baptism of fire? Really?' I manage to chuckle.

Danny glares towards the angel who just shrugs.

'Succubi don't feel any pain. Heightened sexual hunger, but not pain,' Danny says.

I now look towards the angel who gets to his feet and smiles.

'Hey, you needed a little nudge and here you are. But what I said still stands,' he says giving me a meaningful nod.

I'm really too tired to fight them all, not when they are going to all win anyway. My father was right. I could do worse and in time I will love Sebastian like I love Micka and the other Marley woman will be some ancestor I know nothing about. Sebastian would never sleep with a mother and daughter, surely.

'I take it the night went well?' the angel asks.

I really want to punch him in the face.

'Considering the state I found her in, Sebastian, you were sailing rather close to the wind with this one. I nearly fell off my celibate wagon.'

Sebastian takes my arm and pulls me closer so he's holding tight. When I first met Sebastian he had so much power and confidence, but here in this room it's this angel that holds all the cards, but I'm not intimidated. I used to like him a lot. Even in his dated clothes, he seemed a nice guy, but the feelings that have grown over the weeks seem much more deep set.

'You think you could have me?' I challenge moving from Sebastian.

The angel comes towards me.

'Yes, or course I could. If I touched you now, you'd be mine, body and spirit.'

'Try it!'

The whole room is holding its breath and the serpent is rearing its head inside. Sebastian grabs at my hand, but I pull away. They've got to trust me.

'Like I said when I had my hands on you, I prefer to do the chasing.'

'I think you're scared. I think you may have lost your so called touch.'

The angel licks his lips and stepping forward our bodies touch as he looks down at me. His eyes are emerald green and beautifully set off his pale skin. I cannot deny that there is something between us. Something that causes that serpent to stir.

'Fine,' he hisses.

Grabbing me, he places his mouth on mine. I'm surprised by how soft the kiss is. It's like being kissed by feathers. There is no use of the tongue, just lip upon lip. There is no trying to swallow me whole. It's how I'd expect to be kissed by someone who truly loves me. Then something hits and slams me hard. Disgust and hatred fills me. Like a distant memory of betrayal. I wrench away and slap him hard across the cheek.

'That's for the nudge,' I hiss.

Shock is on all faces. They were expecting me to fall at his feet. It's not like I have an angel fetish. The angel recovers himself and fury fills his face as he lifts a hand to return the slap. I wait for the stinging contact, but it doesn't come.

'Don't you dare touch my daughter again, Gabriel.'

I take a step back a little winded. One, my father has stood up for me and secondly the angel I've been communing with and just been swapping salvia with is one of the greatest and powerful angel that ever existed.

'You're never…' I stutter.

'The one and only Miss Marley,' he snaps. 'Well it seems Sebastian that this time you've got one who'll remain faithful. With a hand like that she's all yours.'

Then he disappears. I turn towards the others and give them all a questioning look.

'So who's going to tell me why Gabriel is so interested in me.'

Sebastian

Mina Marley's Online Blog cont…

'Well, who's going first?' I push.

'I should do it. I'm a Marley,' Danny says.

'I'm her father it should be me,' Ray argues.

I take Sebastian's hand and give it a squeeze.

'Sebastian will be my husband. I want him to tell me.'

Sebastian looks down at me a little shocked and Danny and my father wear the same expression.

'Are you sure?' he asks.

'As long as you tell me the truth,' I say.

'I meant about the husband thing,' he smiles.

'If that's okay? I mean if the offer is still on the table.'

'It was never off the table and yes, I will tell you the truth.'

I say my goodbyes to Danny and my father before Sebastian takes my hand and leads to me the library. Sitting down, he takes my hand in his and looks at me for a moment.

'There is something we need to address first,' he says and I find I'm holding my breath. 'It concerns what I said earlier about Marley women.'

Please don't let it be my mother. Please.

'As you may have guessed I have been around a very long time and I told you I had only one wife. Well the truth is that technically I've had two.'

I frown. 'How can you technically have two? Surely you've been married twice or you haven't?' I ask.

'It's a little complicated. Look, Mina, my first wife was a Marley.'

I think the look of relief shows on my face because he frowns.

'You didn't think that the other Marley was your…dear god, Mina what sort of a man do you think I am?'

'So you and my mother never…'

'Maybe it's best I start at the beginning, but you must remember that I love you despite what I am going to tell you.'

I sit back as he talks about his connection with my family.

'My first wife wasn't the one I told you about. My first wife wasn't born a Marley. She became one. She and I were made for each other. Soulmates. But an angel got in the way. They fell in love and I was betrayed. Left alone.

That angel was Gabriel. He should have been punished, but he wasn't and as an appeasement I was given eternal life and the opportunity for a second chance with her descendants. This is because only a Marley woman is meant to be mine and I, hers.

The only problem is that Marley woman are very few and far between. When my second wife came along, I fell madly in love with her as I told you before and you know that story. It was believed she was a Marley, but she was only a distant cousin to your own bloodline.

'Then there was Deanna, she was only seventeen when we met. A child really. She and I just never clicked and you may not know this but she was in love with someone else. So I walked away. I never wanted to force her to love me, because the right one would never be forced, it would just happen.'

I feel I can barely breathe as he talks. Who is this man that I've agreed to marry? And who was this other person my mother loved? Far too many questions for me to process.

'Okay,' I manage to say. 'So why is Gabriel so interested in me now? I'm nothing to do with your first wife.'

'Gabriel and the Marley women are emotionally connected and believes he has a right to any of them.'

'Which explains why you were so nervous when I challenged him,' I say. 'And I suppose the Micka thing wasn't good either.'

'No it wasn't,' Sebastian smiles. 'You seem to be taking this all very well, considering.'

'You know what? This year I've found out I'm a succubus and my family are some really important thing in Hell. Then there are those who want me dead. I think your past is the least of my worries. As for Gabriel...well, he got put in his place with this Marley woman.'

Sebastian grabs holds of me and hugs me tightly.

'I love you so much. You are more than any man could ever ask for.'

Getting to my feet, I pull away from his grasp. I go to where his desk stands and provocatively perch on its edge.

'I believe that we were rudely interrupted,' I say.

A smile spreads across Sebastian's face as he gets to his feet. Walking towards me, he stands between my legs and pushes me onto the desk.

'You are turning into a true flirt Miss Marley.'

With his hands resting on my thigh, I will him to touch me further. He's right. There is a real change in me. I'm fully aware of my sexual power and how to use it. Jono was right, sex is important. The connection is important, more than what the heart offers.

'I want you to have me on this desk right now,' I purr.

Sebastian's eyes widen at my forwardness. He's not used to this from me. But he's known other Marleys. What we become and turn into. Slowly, I reach over and pull him closer and kiss him lightly on the mouth. Using tongue, I tease and lick his lips gently, barely touching. He tries to move close, but I pull away. I want this slowly. Nothing rushed.

Using my thighs, I hold him place, while slowly undo his shirt and run my fingers down his toned torso. He shudders under my touch as I continue my tease.

'What are you trying to do me?' he whispers.

My fingers stop momentarily as a sudden memory using those words floods me. I shake it away. This is different. My fingers continue their mission as they reach his trousers squeezing and touching through the material.

He groans and squirms under my touch. His own hands find my breasts when he pulls my shirt over my head. When his mouth covers my nipples it's my turn to moan and it causes me to squeeze and rub harder.

'Mina, I need too…'

He doesn't finish as he hoists me up so he can pull off my jeans and pants. Just as quickly, I grab and free him. He's inside me in a moment. We are not taking it slow now. Now we are in desperate frantic mode.

I have no idea where Clegg is, but I don't give a damn. I just can't help myself from being noisy. Lifting me up, still joined, Sebastian's not letting me go so easily. One orgasm is not enough. He wants more.

He walks to the bookshelves and pushes my back against them and with my legs still around his waist he continues his thrusting. My name is chanted over and over again. Suddenly another orgasm ripples through me just before his own body tenses and shudders inside me. So intense is his own climax, he nearly drops me, instead we both slide down the bookcases onto the floor exhausted and fully satisfied.

Laid in his lap, we are still half dressed on the library floor. It's nice just to lay and be still and quiet. His fingers stroke my hair and everything seems perfect.

'Would you consider living here with me?' he asks.

I sit up to see his face.

'I would love to, but I need to go back and face everyone in town. No matter what, they all loved Micka and I've behaved badly.'

'You have no reason to explain anything to them and as for Micka, they have no choice but to move on and accept it.'

'Let me stay here another night, because I can't face them all just yet.'

'Stay as long as you want to.'

Sebastian gets to his feet and picks me up off the floor.

'You, Miss Marley need to relax and chill out and so I'm taking you to bed.'

'I wouldn't say no to that,' I smile.

'No, I guess you wouldn't, but some of us need to catch up with work.'

He carries me up to his bedroom and lays me on the bed kissing me quickly on the lips. As he gets to the door a thought suddenly hits me. Something I'd never thought to ask before.

'Sebastian, what exactly do you do?'

He stands in the open door and smiles.

'My work involves furniture,' he says and then he's gone.

Back to Supton

Ray's Journal April 24th 2330hrs

My body shook as I left Sebastian's. I have never stood up to an Archangel and Gabriel of all of them. The common human perception is that Gabriel is the sweetest and kindest of all the Archangels. How so far off the mark they are. He is just as fearsome and dangerous as his brothers. If not more so.

He took what wasn't his and continued to do so. But not this time. This time, he challenged my daughter—my Mina. She took him on and knocked him back. I have never been more proud than I was then.

I know Daniel was nervous, but when she slapped Gabriel, I could almost feel Daniel swell up with pride also. Gabriel was an arsehole to you, Deanna. He was another one that thought you would fall at his feet, but you didn't and so he decreed that you were not the one.

You knew you were damn special. The first pure born girl in near on a thousand years and to be born with a brother was beyond anything. Your mother and father were both from hell and you were brought up from a young age believing that you were destined for greatness. Like your ancestors, you would make the human world great, by giving them yourself.

But then you fell in love. You were seventeen and in the throes of hormones and lust. The attraction was a great one and no one could tear you away, not even Gabriel. When Sebastian came along and walked away it hit you hard. The glory was going to be lost. You swore that no other Marley woman would take your place in greatness.

Years later, when Mina was born, I was told by Uzrel you were devastated, because you knew that she was going to be your successor. She would grow up and take your crown and there were times you found that hard. But no matter what you loved her. That I will always believe.

Now, all I can do is sit back and let be what will be. Mina is a fully fledged Marley woman and her first victim was Micka and there will be more. This town better be ready to receive its queen, because she's going to grab it by its throat and make it bend to her will.

I should feel some sympathy for my fellow angel, Micka. I understand his pain and right now he'll be beyond grief. He needs to move on. Go back home and heal and stay away from this town and Mina.

#

Mina's Online Blog 25th April 2200hrs

Sitting in the back of the Lexus, I look out at the hustle and bustle of Mina's. Jaq, Astrid and Vicky are holding the fort pretty well. Maybe it's time to let this place go and hand it over to Jaq.

Jesus, Jaq! She's going to be majorly pissed at me. But surely she must understand that I had to go. I know I would if it were her. I have to keep Sebastian's words in mind. I'm an adult who can make my own choices. I shouldn't have to explain myself.

Looking down at my new clothes, I sigh. Gone are the boyfriend slouch jeans and Doc Martins, instead I'm wearing tight jeans, a feminine floating, but barely see though top with high heeled boots. I'd asked Sebastian to take me shopping. I need to shed that old Mina to make way for the new. It's amazing how confident I feel in my own skin, but the change is scary too.

Taking a deep breath, I reach for the door handle and step out of the car. Walking through Mina's front door, the whole place silences. Fuck me! It's like last chance saloon. My waitresses stop and stare. None make the move towards me. Fine! If that's what they want. Holding my head high, I walk towards the counter and grabbing the coffee jug, I approach where Mr Jenkins sits.

'You wanting a top up?'

He looks around at everyone else and then back at me nervously.

'That would be great,' he says.

Pouring the coffee, I can feel the tension of the diner rising. Slamming the coffee jug down, I decide that enough is enough. This is my territory and they have to damn well respect me.

'I've no idea what you've all heard on the rumour mill, but here's the truth from the horse's mouth. I ran away with Micka, thinking I loved him. It turns out I was wrong. All those who knew my mother and uncle know what I am. I am a Marley succubus and used Micka for my own pleasure. Now that's over and I'm going to become Mrs Daniels. Now if any of you have a problem with this then I suggest you use the door.'

No one moves and slowly, they continue to eat. I breathe a sigh of relief until I turn and see Jaq's abandoned apron. Astrid and Vicky can't meet my eye. Normally, I'd crave for their approval, but whatever happened to me the past twenty four hours has made me not care. Going out back, I find that Dom and Jaq arguing in whispers.

'Is this a private party or can anyone join in?' I ask.

Jaq turns to look at me and I'm shocked to see fury in her face and a little bit of hatred. Jaq and I have pissed each other off many times, but there's always been a deep love. Now it seems I've pushed our friendship to the limit.

'I don't want to speak to you,' she hisses. 'You disgust me.'

'And pray tell what I've done to offend you?' I say snottily.

'It's not just me. You've fucked off everyone. I never realised how selfish you could be. Leaving us like that was bad enough, but I kinda understood. You loved him, we *all* fucking got that you loved him. But to then run and shack up with The Lord of the Manor...words are beyond me.'

'Well at least he's free for you to have now. After all, you've always wanted whatever I've had. Jono, this place. I even could have had Dom if I wanted to.'

The slap stings my face and before I can react. Dom is in between us in a flash.

'Mina, I'm taking Jaq home. Craig's in the kitchen, he'll cover.'

'Fine, get her out of here,' I snap.

I lock myself in my office and I'm surprised that there's no tears. In fact, I don't feel anything. No guilt or anything. This is strange, but then I'm now Marley and this is what Marleys are all about. I can't stay hidden in here. I have nothing to be ashamed of.

Back at the counter, the usual chatter fills the diner and my remaining waitresses work as though nothing has happened. Vicky is the first to catch my eye as she comes to the counter. A tentative smile forms her on her lips.

'I hope I'm going to get a pay rise, coz I had to put in overtime.'

I can't help, but laugh at her and it eases some of the tension. Next it's Astrid's turn. She's a different kettle of fish to Vicky. She like me is a demon, but I still hold prestige over her.

'Jaq will come round. They all will, but you have to accept that you were selfish.'

'I don't accept anything, Astrid, but being from hell you'll know all about that. I am what I am.'

With a nod of her head, she too continues to work, but the day's not over yet. There is still one more person to go. Someone who hates Sebastian more than most and when I hear the door go, I look up and get a surprise, because it's not who I expect. Candice stands and stares at me and then with a click of her fingers, she goes out back.

Closing my office door behind us, I wait for whatever shit she's going to come out with. I notice that she too is dressed differently. More normal, but still utilising the black.

'You and I need to talk,' she says.

'I don't want to hear it. Who I fuck is none of your business,' I snap.

She frowns at me and then shakes her head.

'You're right.'

My mouth opens to fire something back, but her new attitude has just thrown me off course.

'Look, I'm here because there are a few things you need to know. Like, did you know that we were born at the same time on the same day? Or that we are somehow connected on some serious level?'

'No, why would I know that?' I ask.

She gets to her feet and circles, looking me up and down.

'What the fuck happened to you after the 23rd?' she asks.

'Why what happened to you?' I throw.

I'm not prepared to just divulge everything to her just like that. I want to know if she has changed too and why.

'Lorreli sent me to Faeterrea. She said I needed to be out of the way. Now I've come back and everything feels and seems different. I have control and stillness. I am no longer pissed at everyone, where as you…you just look like someone's polished your ego that much that you think you're invincible.'

She stops for a moment and listens.

'Lorreli wants to know where Micka is?'

As a reflex action, I tense at his name. I know one day I will stop reacting to it, but I wish it was sooner rather than later.

'I don't know,' I manage to say steadily. 'Does it matter now I'm marrying Sebastian?'

'Are you sure you want to do this?' Candice starts asking herself. She listens and then nods.

'Fine, but let me sit down first.' Then to me. 'Lorreli wants to speak to you.'

Before I can protest Candice has sat and in a flash her eyes has changed and so has her voice. This is the first time I've spoken directly to my last remaining godmother and I'm feeling a little freaked.

'Mina, I am Lorreli. I know that this must be a little strange hearing my voice, but there's a reason I've decided to speak now. You and Candice need protecting and that was where Micka was supposed to come in. Your love affair has thrown everything off course and your seduction of Uzrel–Mina, my darling you have well and truly allowed the shit to hit the fan.'

'I'm with Sebastian now,' I say.

'You think that by just being with Sebastian means all this ends. It doesn't. This is just the beginning.'

Slumping onto my chair, I sigh. This is all I need.

'Why can't you all just leave me to get on with it?'

Lorreli sighs and shakes her head.

'Honey, I wish with all my heart that we could. But, you're a Marley and that will never happen.'

'Well fuck that,' I snap getting to my feet. 'Sebastian will make you leave me alone.'

'Listen to yourself, when did you become a spoilt child?' she chastises.

I open my mouth to argue back, but I can see that she's gone as Candice's condescending eyes looks back at me.

'She's not prepared to talk to you when you're like this,' Candice says shrugging.

'Fine. I don't need any of them anymore. I am a Marley.'

'That excuse is not going to work for long. At the end of the day you are no different to the demon that waits your tables,' Candice says.

I watch her leave my office and I fall into my office chair. Why don't they all just leave me alone? I've done what they've asked. What more do they want?

#

Email from Jaq to Carla 25th April 1130hrs

I cannot believe that fucking bitch. She waltzes in to Mina's like she owns the place...well, I know she does, but she waltzes in and tells the lot of us that if we don't like what she's done then to use the fucking door. And to top it off, she tells me that she could have Dom any time she wanted. WTF.

She didn't even care that she not only left this town, but left me too. I had to step up and run Mina's as well as answer every goddamn question that came my way. It was hard. I missed not being able to pick up the phone and call. She fucked up big time and there's no apology for anything. Not even a fucking thank you.

I'm sick to death of all this Marley shit. They are no special to any other demon. It's just that everyone knows their name. Well, I don't care. It's a name.

I've no idea what's happened to my best friend. I don't recognise the woman that claims to be Mina. Even the clothes she's wearing is not hers. Dressed like...well like Lydia. This is Sebastian's doing. He's turning her into what he wants her to be. Well if she wants to be some trophy wife than I'm leaving her to her. I don't need her shit.

#

Candice's Journal 25th April 2115hrs

I can't believe the woman that I've just left in Mina's office. It's like someone has fucking swapped bodies with her. Full of confidence—no not confidence—arrogance. Then Lorreli wanted to talk

27

to her. That's a new development. I'd never let her do that before and it fucking shit me up, but it's got to be done. I don't remember much about it but she must have given Mina grief, because she looked pale once Lorreli was done.

Lorreli has got one of hell a tongue. I've suffered it many times. She's one big character and would hate to take her on in a fight. She must be some sort of badass up there with the angels. But why she doesn't have her own human suit is beyond me.

But Mina's attitude is the real problem, because it's turning into a fucking bad one. She thinks being a Marley will protect her from anything, well it may have worked before, but it won't for much longer. Marleys are nothing but demons. The quicker she accepts that the better it will be.

Anger Management

Mina Marley Online Blog April 30th 2300hrs

The first week back at work has been harder than I ever expected it to be. Jaq still refuses to come to work and the atmosphere is tense at best. I know everyone is thinking that they have to stand on one side or the other, but I don't care. At the end of the day I'm their boss and still Mina. Who I choose to sleep with has nothing to do with it.

This town has always been an opinionated one and I've no idea why I expect it to be any different. I suppose at best, I've always been left alone, but now I am the centre of attention and it's not comfortable.

I may be a succubus, but the stress still gets to me and no matter how hard Sebastian kneads my muscles, I still feel tense. We are both laid in a hot bath. My back against him. Hot steam filling the room.

I've not returned to the flat. In fact, I've not even walked through the front door. There's far too many memories that I'm not ready to face. That flat was my home for three years and I loved it, but in the space of a year someone else came in and polluted that sacred space. Sebastian obviously doesn't care. But I won't commit to saying I will permanently move in with him either. It feels like I'm stuck in limbo with no guide to tell me which way to go.

'What are you thinking about?' Sebastian asks.

'How good your hands feel,' I murmur.

'What about the diner?'

'It's fine.'

I feel him sigh behind me and my body tenses more. Why does he need to know everything that goes on in my head? Sometimes it makes me feel suffocated.

'That's not what I meant?'

I turn in the bath so I'm now facing him. Diversion tactics are needed, because I don't want to face the subject. With my hand wrapped around him and my mouth on his neck, I feel him squirm.

'Mina, please,' he mutters.

'I want you right now,' I whisper seductively.

He groans as my grip tightens and I think I've finally worked my charm when I'm pushed away. Stepping from the bath, he gives me the glorious view of what is truly mine and I pout sulkily.

'What are you doing?' he asks.

'Well if you have to ask then maybe I'm not doing it right.'

'Mina, I want you talk about what's going on at Mina's.'

'I don't want to talk about it. Mina's is my business,' I snap.

'You don't want to talk about it or you don't want to talk about it with me?' he asks.

That damn serpent is on the move once again. I hate the feeling it gives me. It's like a loss of control. Sometimes I wonder if there really is a serpent inside me. It does feel like an animal uncurling and feeding from the inside. All my primal emotions.

'What I want is to make love to my fiancé and not talk about work.'

'I would love for you to make love to me, and we will do, but right now I want to talk about the fact that your best friend has not set foot in the place that you both share.'

'Jaq can do what the fuck she wants. Let the fairy bitch flit her way through life, it's of no consequence to me.'

'But she is important to you.'

'I am important,' I shout.

'Mina, sweetheart. You need to calm down.'

'No, Sebastian, I will not calm down. I am fucking sick to death of everyone treating me like some disobedient child. I am a Marley.'

The serpent was now fully uncoiled inside me and I feel its control. The primal feeling of losing control is strong and addictive. I like how it feels. I want to scream and shout at Sebastian, but I notice that his face pales and he's clutching the bathroom wall.

'Mina,' he whispers.

'What?!'

I follow his eyes down to the bath I'm sitting in and start in shock. The bath water has started to turn to ice. Not cold. But actual pieces of ice in the water. Startled, I jump out of the bath and Sebastian catches me as I slip on the bathroom floor.

'So that's what happened,' I say to Danny, obviously omitting certain details.

After the incident, he was the only one I could think of that would know what was going on. After all he lived with my mother long enough.

Of course Sebastian and I went to bed with tension. I could tell he was scared and that made me uneasy. It doesn't feel good, lying beside a man who fears you. I don't like it, which is why I am sitting at Danny's.

'Well, as far as I know succubi have *some* power over the elements, but obviously not like the Divas. But to be fair, you've not really learned how to control your emotions and right now they are all heightened,' Danny answers.

'Well what do I have to do?'

Danny shrugs. 'Will you listen to me?'

'Of course I'll listen.'

'Because darling, this town talks.'

'And what do they say?'

'Do I really need to tell you?'

I feel that familiar tension once more. I thought Danny at least would be on my side.

'They should mind their own business.'

'Tell me what you feeling right now.'

'Why in hell should I tell you?'

'Because, I don't really want a fire in my house,' Danny nods.

I turn to see that the stove behind us has sprung into life and the heat from the gas burner is burning bright and getting higher.

'I really need you to breathe,' Danny said.

'I am.'

'Then try harder,' he snaps.

I do what he says and slowly the stove goes back to its dead state.

'Now tell me what happens when *That* happens.'

Flopping on the sofa, I shrug. 'It's hard to explain.'

'Try.'

'Well the only way I can explain this is by saying it feels like there's a serpent inside of me and when I get mad it moves and I can't control what it does.'

Danny sits down in front of me and looks me over for a second. His face is pale and can see he's nervous.

'This is when we could do with your fucking angel godparents,' he mutters. 'This serpent as you call it is the combination of the angel and the demon inside. They are both fighting to take control, but you have to command them.'

'And how do I do that? Take mediation classes?'

'You may mock, but you do need to calm down. Succubi are not known for their aggression, yet I can smell it on you like perfume and I've no idea why.'

'Well considering all the shit I've been put through than can you blame me for being angry.'

'No I can't, but do you really want to live like this. With this aggression there's a price, believe me I've paid it.'

'Okay, so what do I have to do?'

'Well it maybe a good idea to get the Divas in just to even things out. Do we have the four?'

I think for a minuite of course there's Nigel and Ann, and there's Florence…

'Yes, but who'se going to talk to Shirley?'

'Christ, is she still going?'

'Yes on the very edge of town where she can't cause anymore fires.'

'Well I guess I best go talk to them,' he says.

I leave Danny's with a promise that we will work together to make this happen. He's right about one thing I do hate feeling like this. I know I'm out of control, but I can do fuck all about it but ride the train.

#

Ray's Journal Journal 1st May 0930hrs

I've just had a visit from Daniel and things are not looking good. He says that Mina is not only affecting her environment, which isn't usually normal, but she is showing signs of increased aggression like an incubus.

I remember when you hit your twenty seventh birthday, your sexual prowess increased tenfold, but you were never aggressive. Seductive, but never violent. You were able to manipulate the elements around you, but nothing like it seems Mina can.

Could it be because she is the Primum?

That thought still makes me shudder and I can already feel every council, royal family and whoever else closing on Supton. She is just as special to them. And then there's the Emandato. They've been suspiciously quiet since Luca. They must be up to something.

'We need to get the Divas,' he says.

I close my eyes in defeat. That means calling on Shirley. Shirley McConnell is the fire Diva with a serious problem with her element. She loves it and is addicted to the heat of what fire can do. She had caused so many problems that when Old Dave's burnt down, she was asked to leave the town. There she lives alone and barely is seen. I think Ann and Nigel look after her and take her what she needs, but the old woman has issues and having her near my daughter doesn't bode well.

Danny is panicking and telling me that Mina needs more work and that she's too dangerous to be left. He's worried about today being the first of May. The day of merriment and sexual adventure. But that's just the Faes. Nothing to do with us or even Mina and I tell him so.

'Her ego will destroy her,' he says.

But what can I do? What is left to do? Surely the Primum is a victim of her own nature. It's the reason we are all what we are. I desperately want to talk to Uzrel, but since Gabriel has shown himself my friend has disappeared.

#

Mina's Online Blog 1st May 2300hrs

It's been a few weeks of barely anyone really bothering me. All peaceful really, even in the diner. People in Supton just get on with things. They have to. It's the only way they can survive. Keep head down and keep going. The good old bury your head in the sand routine.

My exercises with Danny seem to be doing very little and he's just getting exasperated with me. But it's not like I'm not trying. I didn't ask to feel like this. I just can't still myself. He's managed to talk the four Divas into attending and it turned into a bad idea.

Firstly only three of them arrived, Nigel saying that Shirley wanted nothing to do with it. I can't blame her really, whenever there was any fire trouble she'd be hounded and often when Dodds was head of police, she was used as a scapegoat unfairly. So with the three of them and Danny they all try and get me to balance out my elements with little success. I try with all my might, but Danny's tiny flat becomes a haven for all the elements and it's starting to look like carnage.

'She's off balance.'

We all turn and see Shirley standing in the doorway and suddenly, I do feel the balance returning slowly just by her presence.

She's around the same age as Nanna Christine, but where Christine was glamour, Shirley is someone holding onto her youth with an ironclad grip. The jeans she wears is tight fitting, with a small top, that shows a pierced belly button on a surprisingly toned stomach.

'I thought you didn't want to help?' Danny asks.

'Yeah, well I changed my mind. It's kind of hard to ignore things when the elements are all out of sync. I feel like I'm being pulled in all directions, so let's do this.'

So with all four Divas, they all try and balance every element that is torrent inside me. Five hours and nothing but exhaustion and the Divas agree that it's beyond even their control, much to Danny's frustration.

At home, the sex between Sebastian and I is increasing and growing even more aggressive. So much so that Sebastian is struggling to keep up with my demands. Part of me feels bad, but for the most part, I don't care. Sebastian worked damn hard to get me and now he has, he needs to learn to live with the Marley I am.

Today, I'm working at Mina's, because there at least I feel calm. It is Beltaine and another holiday celebration for the Faes. It means very little to me. Jaq used to tell me it was just an excuse for the adults to get frisky with each other. An idea that used to freak us out.

Anyway, the place is ticking away nicely. It's not too busy and so I only have Astrid, out front with me and Craig in the kitchen. I'm not stupid, we are all smiles and hellos, but tension is still an undercurrent. They want Jaq back and that feeling is exemplified every day Dom arrives for a shift, but it's not for me to apologise. But apart from that I'm actually finding being here therapeutic.

Then, the door opens and in he walks. I can already tell by the look on his face he's pissed off at me. My back stiffens ready for whatever he's going to throw.

'Mina,' he mutters.

'Stan,' I answer.

'Are you okay? I heard you had a bad time on your birthday?'

He's up to something. There's no lecture about Sebastian. He hates him with a passion and is not one to keep his opinions to himself. So why is he being so nice?

'It was tough going, but I'm doing okay now.'

'That's good, and are you living at the Manor now?'

Here we go.

'Unofficially, I'm not happy living here at the moment.'

Tannini nods and gives me a smile.

'Fair enough. I may as well have some food while I'm here.'

'There's nothing else, you want to say to me?' I ask.

'Can I get a beer with it?' he smirks.

So he's playing games with me. Fair enough. I take his order and pour the beer and leave him to it. In fact, I'm actually glad he's not nagging at me. It always gets me moody and I've enough anger management issues as it is without causing some in my own diner.

Then suddenly, there's some commotion from outside. Everyone is on their feet and moving nervously towards the door, but I'm not scared. I've faced much worse. I push them out the way. A black limousine pulls up and my first thought is Jono, but he would have called. Tannini is at my side and he looks my way nervously. The door opens and out steps the most beautiful woman I've ever seen followed by an equally stunning man. Both look almost Amazonian. Everyone in the street stares at them open mouthed until those that are Weres lower themselves onto bended knee.

'What the hell?' I mutter.

'Mina, go inside and ring your father and Sebastian,' Tannini whispers.

'Why?'

'Just fucking do it.'

His tone causes me to obey and quickly turn on my heel and hurry inside. As I pick up the phone, Tannini grabs it off me. I didn't realise he'd followed behind so close.

'Change of plan. Go up to the flat.'

I turn away from my desk and frown at him. Now I'm getting bossed around? Go inside. Go upstairs. Make up your mind. It's not like Tannini to be so aggressive, but because he is, that makes me nervous.

'I don't want to.'

'Mina, don't make me carry you up there. Fucking go.'

I go to the door where the stairs are and stand and stare at them for a moment. I don't want to go up. I can't go up. I'm not ready.

'Mina, I said get the fuck up there,' Tannini hisses.

'No, I'll go in my office.'

Slamming the stair door shut, I go to my office chair and sit and wait. A moment later, Tannini enters and looks me over.

'They're on their way,' he says.

'And are you going to tell me why I'm hiding in here? And who the fuck, the power couple are out there?'

'You know that each of us have our own big wigs,' he says and I nod. 'Well those out there are the fucking Lunarites and they are wanting you.'

'Great, what the fuck have I done to them?'

My office door opening stops Tannini from answering and my father enters the room. How in hell did he get here so quick?

'Sebastian has asked them to go the Manor,' he says. 'Why are you not upstairs?'

'Because she's being a drama queen about it,' Tannini answers.

'I just didn't want to go upstairs. It's not a crime is it?' I snap.

'Stan, can you leave us?'

He nods leaving my father and I alone. He's lost so much weight in just a few weeks and I've been so wrapped up in myself that I haven't bothered to check on him.

'Mina, honey, there's something else I need to tell you.'

'Go on,' I say.

'I'm not sure how else I can put this, but the Lunarites are not the only elder group that are going to come here and they are coming for you.'

'You mean like the Emandato?'

Fear creeps up my spine. I can't do that again. Luca was too strong and I barely survived. If it hadn't been for Micka and he's gone.

'No, not like the Emandato. They are not here to kill you, but we are not taking any risks.'

'What do they want then? Or am I going to get lied to again?'

'Sebastian wants to talk to you about it,' my father says.

'When did you start taking orders from Sebastian?' I ask.

He gives me a small smile and grabs my arm.

'We'll go out the back way and Mina, you will need to go back to the flat very soon.'

'Why is it so important?'

'Because it's your home and home is where your heart is.'

'What does that mean?'

'It means that right now, you need to go to Sebastian.'

'Fine!'

Soon, I am in Sebastian's room waiting to be called, feeling like a fucking prisoner. The Lunarites are downstairs with my father, Sebastian and Danny, no doubt talking about me. After arriving, I was ushered straight to the bedroom by Clegg, without a word. Now they are all talking without me. I'm getting seriously pissed off. I can speak for myself and what's with the secrets again. I thought we were past it. Annoyed, I grab at my bag to pull out my phone to send some pissy text to Sebastian, and the book *The Boy* falls out onto the floor. Micka's last words come back to me. Picking it up, I decide to look at it once again.

Flicking through the pages, it looks just the same as before. The same damn old story. I sit on the edge of the bed and look at it over and over again. What did Micka mean to read it again? The story told me what I was. What else could there be to it?

The bedroom door opens and I throw the book back into the bag as Sebastian enters.

'I'm really sorry sweetheart.'

'What for? Leaving me up here like some petulant child?' I snap.

'We...I'm not treating you like a child. We are just trying to protect you. We don't want you just wading in with otherworldly elders and making things worse,' Sebastian says sitting down beside me.

'I'm quite capable of handling myself,' I mutter.

'I know and that's what I told Ray and Daniel. But tact is really needed here. Come, I'll take you down to meet Morton and Isabelle.'

'Who?'

Sebastian smiles as he pulls me to my feet.

'Be respectful. They are not used to the way things are done here.'

Entering the living room with Sebastian holding my arm, all eyes turn towards me. Sebastian, had quickly filled me in while I changed. I'd decided that if I was to make a good impression I'd put on something smarter.

The Lunarites are from a royal line that dates back to the very first Weres. Back when the human race was still young, a pair of children was born during what is now known as the Great Cycle. One was a black puma and the other an albino wolf. The tribe soon realised that these animals that regained their human forms were blessings from the Powers that Be. The children became objects of power and soon a new race was bred from those children.

Obviously, breeds have come from being bitten and attacked other the centuries. This Morton and Isabelle are the only ones descended from that pure bloodline and you can tell they know their importance. Arrogance oozes off them and they look at me with little distaste and my own hackles rise.

'Miss Mina, we must apologise for dropping in on you like this. Forgive us, but it was important that we came to see you for ourselves.'

'Well have I met expectations?' I snap.

Isabelle gives me a small smirk, but Morton flinches at my tone and looks pissed at me. In fact, why is no one telling me off? My father and Daniel are just sitting quietly, which is disturbing in itself.

'You have been known to us for a while,' Morton says with controlled calmness.

'Well then there's no need to be here if you know everything,' I throw.

'It seems that a few things were wrong. We'd heard that you were a kind and loving woman who was looked up to. All I see is an egotistical spoilt child.'

'How fucking dare you,' I start to shout.

The ground beneath us rumbles slightly and I feel Sebastian's grip tighten. Isabelle moves towards me, leaving Morton's side.

'Forgive my brother, he has no way with women. Let's you and I go out and walk round the gardens. Leave the gentlemen to their testosterone.'

'I'm not sure it's a good idea,' Sebastian says.

'Mr Daniels, Miss Marley will be safe with me,' Isabelle reassures.

Nodding, I agree and we both leave the men and step into the gardens. It's nice warm spring day and with the buds starting to burst open. The gardens haven't felt more relaxing. Honestly, I barely spend any time in the gardens. There's been no time to and it's a shame, because they are very beautiful. We walk in silence for a while until we come to the ornate statue that I found the first night I broke in. Finding a small bench, we both sit down.

Isabelle is a very beautiful in an exotic way. She reminds me a little of Micka and that causes my insides to twinge. Her clothes are expensive, probably one of a kind. Money is no object. Just like in Sebastian's world.

'Is Morton really a brother or is it one those community things?' I ask.

Isabelle smiles. 'Yes, we are blood, but there's nothing weird between us. We both have partners, but he can get a little intense sometimes.'

'Really, I hadn't noticed,' I smirk. 'So what is the deal? Why me?'

'You know now you are very special. Marley women are rare.'

'What about my mother?'

'Deanna was more than perfect, but she was not you.'

'I'm nothing special, but I suppose Sebastian thinks differently.'

'Sebastian is far too protective for his own good. You really have caught him.'

My back stiffens as I see affection in her face and jealousy pulls at my stomach.

'Well I'm told we are meant for each other,' I say.

'Yes you are. Look, Mina, I hate to be blunt with you, but you do know that you're special? You don't need anybody to tell you that. The fact that you're half and half means that you've got a lot of power and a hell of a lot of influence. Other Elders are going to want to see you.'

'But why?'

'That is not for me to tell you, but know that my people don't mean you any harm. All we wanted was to make sure that you survived the Day of the Dragon.'

'And nothing to do with whether I ended up in Sebastian's bed and not Micka's,' I say far too defensively.

Isabelle gets to her feet and starts to pick at the leaves on the manicured shrub. She looks hurt and suddenly I feel bad. Why I don't want to upset her I've no clue. She's a stranger to me, but I do feel a connection.

'I'm a woman who has loved and lost. I know what it's like to have to make a choice and have my heart broken.'

It takes me a moment for it to dawn on me who she is referring to. Who broke her heart.

'Were you and Sebastian...?'

She now looks my way and then past me and I turn to see the men coming our way. A moment passes as Sebastian catches Isabelle's eye and I take that time to stake my claim, wrapping my arms around him.

'Isabelle and I will be staying nearby. We may well call the other elders together and get this done,' Morton says.

'I'm not being disrespectful, but Mina is a Marley you need to remember that,' Danny adds.

'You throw that name around like it's supposed to put us in our place. I don't care if you're related to Lucifer himself, we do what we have to. You don't rule us,' Morton snaps.

Whatever the guys have been talking about, the atmosphere is still tense. Even after everyone leaves and goes home.

Later that evening, curled up on the sofa, after yet another passionate session, I approach what was discussed with Isabelle.

'Isabelle seems lovely. Her brother is a bit of a nutcase, but she's nice.'

'They live very differently to a lot of their people. Many Weres have never met them. They deal with the Were Council instead,' Sebastian murmurs lazily playing with my hair.

'She's pretty,' I push.

Sebastian sighs beneath me, but doesn't fall for my trap.

'Did you sleep with her?' I ask.

'Where in hell did that come from?'

He moves so he is now on top. Looking down on me.

'She said something about having her heart broken and I'm guessing you were the one that broke it.'

'I have lived a very long time, Mina and I won't apologise for having a sex life, I'm only human.'

'You were lovers?' I ask.

'Yes, we were, but she was married and it was complicated.'

'How long has it been over?'

'A year...Mina wait.'

I push myself from under him and grab my clothes. She must really hate me.

'Did you leave her for me?' I demand.

'Does it matter? It was before you and I,' he says.

'Did you love her? Do you still love her?'

'You are being silly, Mina. After all I've done to get you, you ask me stupid questions like that.'

He pulls me back into a hug and I soften against him. He's right. I shouldn't feel jealous or insecure. He's invested far too much in me.

'I'm sorry,' I mutter.

'You are my woman. I love you and the sooner I get a ring on your finger the better I'll feel.'

The Coming of the Elders

Mina's Online Blog 7th May 2330hrs

First the Lunarites came and slowly day by day other elder are starting to come to town. Every resident is on edge, because it's like having the boss turn up. All we need is *The* Big Boss to arrive. That would spice things up.

The Were Council arrived the following day after the Lunarites and then came the Shifters Council. The only elder not to come were the Faerie King and Queen, but they sent a representation called Morag.

Each elder moved into the town and all asked to see me, but Sebastian is refusing for now. He wants my godparents on side, but so far not even Uz has made his presence known.

I haven't thought about Uz since my birthday and feel angry that's he's just abandoned me. So what if I kissed him. Get a grip and move on. But on top of that I miss him. I need his stability. I decide to see if I can call him. But he won't come to the Manor so standing in my office, I call out my guardian's name.

No answer.

'Uz, you son of a bitch, I need you.'

Still nothing. Sighing, I leave my office and as I do, the door to the staircase opens by itself. I smile. Of course. I get the hint.

'I'm not going up there, you can fucking come down here.'

I get no answer. Fine! It's not like I need him anyway. He can sulk all he likes.

'Is he not answering your call?'

I jump at the sudden voice and turn to see Gabriel leaning against my office door.

'What do you want?'

Giving me a broad smile, he walks back into my office and find myself following. Closing the door, I watch as Gabriel sits down in my chair. Still as arrogant as ever.

'Take a seat,' I say smartly.

He gives me a smile. 'Thank you, I will. Right, Mina, what are we going to do with all these Elders?'

'Why you asking me? You're Gabriel, you should know all the answers,' I say.

'You really are a character Mina,' he answers. 'As anyone told you why they're so interested in you?'

'Why would they do that? It's not like people are throwing information at me.'

Gabriel gets to his feet and looking serious all of a sudden and my body tenses. I'm not sure how to a handle a serious Gabriel.

'Uzrel is no good for you at this moment and he won't come either. I am all you've got.'

'Great,' I mutter.

'Tell Sebastian to gather the Elders and we'll give them what they need.'

'And what is it they need?'

Gabriel touches my cheek and find I don't even flinch, instead I go into the touch.

'The Marley woman, who will give this world what it needs.'

'And that…?'

'Would be telling,' he smirks.

Sebastian took some convincing to allow the Elders into the Manor and even more convincing to have Gabriel there.

'Where is Uzrel?' he demanded.

'He's not answering my call, but Gabriel has offered and we may as well get this over and done with.'

So here we are inside the ballroom at the Manor with all the Elders, Candice and Morag. Their eyes are on both Sebastian and I, until Gabriel enters the room. There's a murmur of surprise. They didn't expect an Arch to be here. The angels are never welcome with any of the Others. It's a them and us mentality.

Gabriel seems to have ditched his Levi Advert look for now and wears a black pinstriped suit and I hate to admit it, but with the copper hair, he looks mighty fine. I tear my gaze away, because I can't do that. Gabriel is way out of my stratosphere and any emotional link felt is not wise to pursue.

Everyone in the room is nervous and Sebastian grabs my hand. I've never felt so much tension in one room before and it seems a life time ago that I was last in here dancing with Micka...no Uz...oh you know who I mean. Gabriel smiles my way before taking centre stage and Sebastian's grip tightens.

'Elders, may I welcome you to Supton and I'm sure Mr Daniels will join me in apologising for making you wait so long for this meeting. But Miss Marley's safety is paramount as you can agree.'

'You know why we are here, Master Gabriel, but it seems Miss Marley is clueless...'

'I'm not clueless,' I snap out.

The speaker, who I think is one of the Shifters Council looks taken aback and feel Sebastian squeeze my hand. The shifter is a woman a little older than I and tall. Her dark hair is tied neatly and with her suit looks almost pristine. I've seen her talking to Tannini and that's how I know she's a Shifter and she's here with an older much thinner gentleman.

'Forgive me, Miss Marley, I didn't mean you were clueless,' she says. 'I'm Beverley Carson and a representative of the Shifters Council.'

She moves towards me with a held out hand. Her face is filled with warmth and I realise that she's telling the truth. She's actually trying to stick up for me and I've no idea why. Moving away from Sebastian, I take her hand and shake it.

'Nice to meet you, I'm sorry for snapping,' I offer.

'It's fine,' she smiles and goes back to her companion. 'It would be nice if the men were a little upfront.'

'They are men, what do we expect,' I whisper and she laughs.

Gabriel comes to my side and places an arm around my shoulder and from the corner of my eye, I note Sebastian stiffening, especially since I don't shrug it off.

'So is anyone going to tell me what this is all about? I ask.

No-one speaks for a moment and I feel self-conscious standing there.

'Well, is no-one going to answer the girl?' Gabriel says. 'You've come all this way and you won't answer her question.'

'Is she the Primum and if she is, where is our queen?' Morag says.

Gabriel's hand clenches my shoulder and I hear Sebastian take an intake of breath.

'You all know the legacy of the Marley and Mr Daniels. I know that the Cycle Glorious has just passed and that's caused you to be twitchy. As for you Fae, you need to give up on this idea of your queen coming back,' Gabriel said.

I see both Morag and Candice bristle. I have no idea who this queen is, but it seems pretty damn important. Also, what on earth is a Primum. Sounds like some Transformer toy.

'With respect, Master, the signs are there and you cannot deny your sister existed,' Morag pushes.

Gabriel's hand leaves my shoulder and something about his body language makes me go and sit with Sebastian. I look at him and all I get is a small shake of the head.

'Please don't presume to tell me what I should or should not believe about my family,' Gabriel answers coldly.

'I presume nothing, *Master,* but *our* Mother will return to us and you know full well why. You were there.'

Like a flash, Gabriel has Morag by the throat and everyone gasps out loud. Even Candice has taken a step back.

'If you ever talk to me about my sister again I will snap your pretty little neck in two,' he hisses.

Finally letting go, he walks back to where he started and I notice the flexing of knuckles. He's a scary son of a bitch when angry and they all know it. This archangel has a hell of a lot a power. But the Fae doesn't seem to want to give up as she pushes through the crowd.

'You've not answered the question,' she pushes.

'Because I'm choosing not to.'

'And the Primum?' Morag asks.

'Is not your concern.'

My heart feels like it's about to drop out of my chest as a breeze flutters behind me. It's been so long since I've heard his voice and I'm shocked that it still has an effect on me and to make things worse Sebastian knows it too as he looks my way.

'What are you doing here Militant?' Gabriel snaps.

'Sebastian specifically asked for a godparent to be here with Mina during this meeting and I am still her godfather,' Micka says.

Now Sebastian gets to his feet and moves between Micka and me.

'You are not what I asked for. She told you to leave,' he says.

'I am her godfather and have a duty to protect her,' Micka insists.

'You're not her guardian,' Sebastian snaps.

I watch as the two men argue with each other and something strange starts to happen. Everything distorts and twists and deep inside that serpent starts to uncoil. But this time it's different. This time I know that once it uncoils I am gone. No amount of fucking Sebastian will make this stop and throwing my head back, I scream out loud and succumb to the Marley nature.

Every being in that room silences as I run from the room. Slamming myself into the bedroom the changes are taking my breath away. How dare Micka just turn up? How dare any of them try and rule me. I am a Marley and a queen.

Then I see it. The book on the bed. Not where I left it, but nothing surprises me anymore. Someone out there wants me to see this. Really see it. As I step closer the pages come to life and as I pick it up I see for the first time what's beneath the story.

What Micka wanted me to see and I now know my story and I'm floored.

The serpent is fully uncoiled and my body tightens from the inside and it brings me to my knees. I can't do this anymore. It's time for me to give in and let go.

Ray's Journal 8th May 0830hrs

I thought that I'd experienced the worst time with Mina during the cycle, but nothing prepared me for this. I'm not sure what tipped her over the edge. My inclination is to blame Micka, but then the elders were talking about the Primum, maybe that's what happened. We should have been honest from the beginning with her, but we haven't and again paying the price. Now Mina is on the rampage somewhere and no-one can find her. We've scoured the town looking for her and now we've no choice but to go to the city.

Daniel is not helping matters. He keeps insisting that this isn't normal. She shouldn't be so out of control. We already know this, but it doesn't help us find her. Micka and Sebastian stand in my home with Gabriel. The three of them all look shifty. For once they all have something in common. They all love Mina, and hate each other equally, but they need to pull together.

I've spent years afraid of Sebastian and Gabriel, but with Mina missing fear is long out of the window. I'm ready to fight them all for my daughter and they are surprised that I have already shouted at them. But I need to concentrate on one person.

'What made you appear from nowhere?' I ask Micka getting him alone.

'I didn't want to. It was the hardest thing I've ever had to do returning here,' he answers.

'You mean you went back?' I ask.

'Mina broke my heart,' he says. 'There was no other choice, but the Powers demanded I return. They don't want her to know she's the Primum. They're sending messages out to the Elders and telling them to back off.'

'Why would they do that? They all have an interest if she's the Primum.'

'It's not if, Ray, it is. Mina is the Primum and right now...'

'That Primum is unleashed somewhere,' I finish. 'Danny,' I shout.

Danny hurries into my bedroom where Micka and I are holed up.

'You need to tell him?' I say.

Micka repeats what he's told me and to my surprise Danny sits on the bed and looks winded.

'So it's true, she's more than just a Marley?' he asks.

'Does Sebastian know?' I ask.

Micka shrugs his shoulders. 'The reason he rejected Deanna was because he was told she was not the one. He must know.'

'And it's clear that he loves her more than the other one. The chemistry is evident, I add.

I see Micka flinch, but he tries to hide it. I know his pain. I know it damn well.

'What about Uzrel?' I ask.

'He won't come. He's scared of her and of himself,' Micka answers.

That's fair enough I suppose. He was pushed beyond the boundaries and must be finding it hard to fight back.

'We need to find her, because if the Emandato get wind that she's on the loose it's over,' I say.

No-one answers. No solution. My poor daughter. They have led her like a lamb to the slaughter and I'm powerless.

Later that evening, everyone has left me alone while they continue the search. This gives me time to do what I never thought I'd ever do. If she is indeed the Primum, there's nothing I can do about it. The Powers control that and I am sure if they put more effort in, they would find her. But Mina is a Marley and there's one person other than Daniel who can add to the pot. I say person, but I use the term loosely. I don't even think he'll come, but I've no choice. Needs must. I have what I need to call. Somewhere in this house.

Going down to the basement where I've prepared the ritual. This house is purpose built for its position in this town and for the first time since it was built, I am about to put its position to the test. Taking the notes, I've copied from *The Boy*. The hidden passages that Mina has not yet found. Although in her current state then she must know soon how to read that blasted book.

I've never felt so scared and it's not helping that I was once an angel. He hates angels, but I hope that he still has an interest in the Marleys to want to help. In my hand is the offering, because nothing ever comes for free. The offering of choice is the blood of a lamb, because it's all about purity. It's always about purity. Spilling it on the consecrated circle I begin the chant.

Mina

Ray's Journal 9th May 2230hrs

I wake up to the sun shining in my face from the bedroom window. How did I get here? The last thing I remember was being in the basement and now I'm here. Shifting position, my head pounds. It's like I've been on the ale with Stan all night. The room spins and I flop back onto the bed.

'What were you trying to do?'

I sit up straight in bed once more and groan.

'Uzrel, where have you been?'

'That's not important. Ray, you've done a stupid thing. How could you do that to Mina?' Uzrel snaps.

'Did he come?' I ask.

'He was making you suffer. It's a good job that I stepped in otherwise Mina would be burying a parent,' Uzrel says sitting on the edge of the bed. 'You look like shit by the way.'

'But did I manage to summon him?' I demand.

'Ray, leave Mina to us. You don't need him. We will find her.'

'And have you found her?'

Uzrel gets to his feet and moves around my room. I already know the answer.

'We think she may have gone to the city.'

'So what's made you come out of the woodwork? Micka said that you had washed your hands of her,' I ask.

'We have a problem, the Emandato are looking for her too. We've had a tip off,' he says. 'And I would never wash my hands of Mina. I just needed some time.'

The fog in my head disappears instantly. I knew that their lack of action after Luca was too good to be true. But they are good at what they do. Like any good hunter they were waiting for the right time and now Mina is out there somewhere and vulnerable.

'You should have let me finished the ritual,' I snap getting out of bed.

'Yes because calling *That* up from the pits would have helped matters.'

'It's better than sitting here and waiting for her.'

'Then pack a bag. You and I are going to the city.'

#

Jaq's Email to Carla 27th May 0930hrs

I don't know if you've heard the news about Mina's disappearance. I'm sure mum and dad have been in touch. If you hear anything or she comes to you. Let me know first. Please. I will tell Jono, who's out there looking too.

Much Love

Jaq

Ray's Journal 28th May 2300hrs

We've finally found her. It's taken us nearly three weeks, but we've finally found Mina.

It's not over by a long shot, but at least we've got her somewhere safe for now at least.

We are all in some serious shit and my actions have not made things easier just as Uzrel predicted.

Uzrel and I went to the city and convened with Sebastian, Daniel and Gabriel. Daniel had tried to contact Jonathan, but even he'd dropped off the map. This was worrying. The two of them together. In the state that Mina was in was asking for trouble.

Both Micka and Gabriel with Uzrel bounced back and forth trying to track her and they were getting nowhere. Even Candice tried with Lorreli, but Mina was blocking their progress. How I had no idea. She didn't want to be found. But then word came of a couple matching Jonathan and Mina's description somewhere at the other side of the city known as Hades Hole. I actually can't believe we've not thought of looking there.

Hades Hole is a notorious hotspot for Others who do not live within the rules of the human world. Renegades if you like. It's a dangerous place to be and it sickens me that my daughter has been staying there. Sebastian of course was furious when he found out.

'What has possessed her? I thought that once we... after her birthday we would be fine. She would be fine.'

'You knew deep down that this could happen,' Daniel said.

'Because she's the Primum? But this didn't happen last time,' Sebastian argued back.

'You didn't have her back then,' Gabriel added.

The three men continued to argue and blame each other for her actions, but they have all forgotten that whether Mina is the Primum or not or even a Marley. She is Mina. My daughter with a heart of gold that is struggling with a new nature. She may be an incarnation, but it doesn't mean that she's the same. I scream at them to shut up and Sebastian has the last word.

'I will marry her as soon as I damn well can and put an end to this charade.'

And how can we argue with that, although I have no idea what putting a ring on her finger will achieve. She is who she is.

But then we got the information and all of us went to find both my daughter and nephew, and we were in for a shock.

We walked the streets and felt repulsed at our surroundings. There was desperation in the air and other repulsive smells. However, there is something to be said about walking these streets with angels. We were watched keenly, but not approached. Seeing the state that some of those lost Others distressed me. Many had no doubt come into my care and this could be what happened to them. Why weren't their leaders helping them out? That's what they are there for.

Supton is not the only town that does what we do, although ours is much more open than others. Ex-angels that are repentant are used as I am, to rehabilitate Others into the human world. The majority of them live in human towns where the so called angel holds some power. A mayor or politician. Someone with the capabilities to form contacts and put these Others into the world unseen. I have been in contact with some of the other towns on occasion, we at Supton are like the mother ship. The place they all want to be, but in all honesty, you have to be pretty damn special to be placed in our town. The angels can be very picky and now my Mina has joined those that are abandoned. One of the places she's in most danger.

Finally in a desolate room, in some rundown house, we found Jonathan looking a little worse for wear.

'If you've touched my wife then you will pay boy,' Sebastian hissed.

Daniel stepped between them and pushed Sebastian away.

'She is no-one's wife and touch my son again and it will be you who will pay.' Daniel hissed. 'Where is she?

'Believe me, I would have called earlier, but I didn't dare leave her alone. She's hotter than a volcano,' Jonathan defended.

'Then why can't we feel her?' Daniel asked.

'Because I've found a way to bind her to stop her scent spreading,' Jonathan answered.

He took us towards a door, which was bolted shut and I could feel the tension coming from everyone.

'I should go in?' I say. 'I'm her father and less likely...'

'I'm going to be her husband,' Sebastian snapped.

'Exacty, she'll eat you alive in there,' Jonathan added.

'Did you?' Daniel asks the question we are all thinking.

Jonathan collapses against the door. He looks beyond himself as though he's been fighting twenty men.

'I swear I never touched her, but I wanted to. Physically I craved for her and for that I've had to punish myself.'

'What do you mean punish yourself?' I ask.

With no words, he slowly lifted his shirt and we saw the scars of where a knife had cut deeply into skin. Both Danny and I cussed. The poor boy.

'Well at least you were able to control yourself,' Sebastian said with little sympathy.

We argued, but one of us had had enough and the door had been smashed open and Daniel was inside the room where all we heard was the word fuck. The sight as we entered the room stilled each of us and I could tell Jonathan was nervous at what he'd resorted to do.

In the middle of the room was a small bare bed with a white duvet on it. There was nothing visible restraining Mina to the bed, but the symbols on the walls, ceiling and floor held her in place. Luckily Daniel had the sense not to step into the charmed space.

My daughter there on the bed looked as demonic as she could possibly be. Pure hell surrounded her aura. The Marley taking her over. Her red hair was matted to her head and her body barely clothed in one of Jonathan's shirts, making me wonder where her clothes were.

'Daddy,' she squealed sitting up on the bed.

'How did you learn to do this?' Daniel asked.

'A demon who owns a shop further down the street gave me what I needed. Cost me half my bank balance,' Jonathan answered.

'Uncle Danny,' Mina purred uncurling her body.

'We need to get her home,' Sebastian pushed.

'All my men in one room. What am I to do?' Mina played.

Sebastian made a move towards her, but was stopped by an invisible force.

'It's the charm,' Jonathan says. 'I made it that neither she can get out or no-one can get to her.'

'Then break it and let me get her,' Sebastian snapped.

'I'm not breaking anything until we control her,' Jonathan hissed.

'She will be my wife...'

'But she's not yet. Jonathan is right,' Daniel added.

'She is mine. I will control her,' Sebastian argued.

Daniel laughed at this. "You fool, you could never control her. That's why we are here now.'

The three of them continued to argue and that's when it happened. The smell was the first thing to hit me and then came the change in the air. The air of power and pure hell.

'He's coming,' Mina chanted.

'Who's coming,' Sebastian snaps, just as the word fuck leaves mine and Daniel's.

'I am.'

And there he is in all his hellish glory, if I can use such a word to describe the father of my daughter's bloodline.

Marleux

Tannini's Journal 30th May 2330hrs

When Beverley told me what happened at the Manor, I didn't quite believe it. She told me of how the Faes pushed Gabriel into telling them of their Great Mother and if Mina was the Primum, and how at that moment Micka had appeared.

'And that's when it truly kicked off,' Beverley said. 'Mina just started screaming and it was like every element was fusing together in one place. I had to fight not to shift there and then.'

Then, Mina disappeared. Just like that. Ray of course came to me for help, but I had to refuse, because the Council wanted to see me. Beverley and I travelled to the city where the Council waited.

There we, well I mean Beverley, told them that it wasn't confirmed whether Mina Marley was the Primum, but Beverley wasn't in any doubt.

It seems my love has made a lifetime of studying the Primum and her return. This was just as much as fucking shock to me. When I asked her why the interest, she merely answered that it was far more interesting than our stories, which I don't blame her for.

The power felt when Mina lost control are all pointers and signs that she is the Primum. But why is this Primum so important to us Others? It's something I've never cared to know, but now I need to.

All Otherworldlies have their roots. Their first mothers and fathers. However, the Primum allowed us the freedom to walk amongst the humans. It was her actions that separated us from the Powers that

Be hold. The reason we don't answer fully to the angels. Why do we care now if we have our freedom? Well, because every time the Primum graces us with her presence she gives the world her greatest gift and in doing so, her greatest sacrifice. It's her way of telling the Powers that Be that they cannot control everything. That we are all free. Other or human.

That is the reason every Otherworldly elder is scrambling to know for certain if Mina is the Primum, so that we can know for certain if her gift will be in our lifetime. Thinking of my adopted niece in this way plays with my fucking head.

Now I've heard news that disturbs me and others more. Mina has been found safe. Fuck, that's not the news. The news is that Ray in his own stupidity and desperation has summoned Marleux and the bastard has risen his ugly head from the pits. This ain't going to end well for Mina or anyone. That demonic bastard is going to want payment.

#

Ray's Journal 30th May 2200hrs

'I am taking her back to hell,' Marleux states.

He stands there all high and mighty and with his presence I feel sickness. The others do too. I can see it. Daniel and Jonathan have both bowed their heads instinctively. They know deep in their blood who it is.

'You can't,' I manage to say.

'Then why summon me?'

'You summoned him?' Sebastian spits.

'I was desperate,' I snap. 'We...I need your help.'

He may look like a human man and the resemblance to Danny is astounding. The same dark hair and bright green eyes. Even has the decency to wear a black suit. But he is as pure as it comes and there's nothing but pure hell around him. The problem is that now I've summoned him, I'll have to find a way to put him back in the box.

'And why would I do that? Marleux asks.

'Because she is of our blood,' Daniel whispers.

Marleux walks towards my daughter and to my surprise, she flinches away from him in fear.

'I can see that she's of my blood and a mighty fine specimen too. I hear she's the Primum, which makes her a perfect playmate in hell. So I'm taking her.'

Sebastian rushes forward only to be hit by the protective force-field.

'You will not touch her.'

Marleux laughs as Sebastian lands on the floor at my feet.

'What *are* you calling yourself these days?' Marleux chides.

'Sebastian Daniels,' Sebastian answers getting to his feet.

'Very modern and up your own arse.'

I find it hard not to smile and so is Daniel. Marleux maybe evil, but he's also very perceptive.

'Tell me Sebastian, at what point does my family and you stop being entwined? Because I, quite frankly, am bored with all this shit.'

'I was promised...'

'I don't give a rat's arse what you were promised boy. The girl is of my blood and if I want to take her then I fucking well will.'

'Please, don't,' I start to beg as Marleux moves towards my daughter.

There's pure fear on her face and I can't let him drag my baby girl to the pits of hell to be his little toy.

'Do something,' I hiss at Daniel, but it's Jonathan that makes the move.

Jumping past Marleux and in front of Mina he reaches above their heads and smashes at the markings on the ceiling at the same time screams words that send shivers down my spine. But I have to admire that it takes some balls to speak those words. The room fills with white light and I breathe a sigh of relief as Marleux screams and that's the last we see as all of us disappear.

The Primum

Ray's Journal's Cont…

'Thank the Powers you pay attention,' Uzrel says as he lays a now unconscious Mina onto Sebastian's bed.

'Don't ask me why, but I knew you were there waiting,' Jonathan answered.

We have been transported by the three angels back to Supton and the Manor and Micka is already working on protecting it from Marleux.

He's going to be mighty pissed off that we've taken her from beneath him and even more so that I summoned him for no reason. I cannot believe I was that stupid.

'You've certainly got a big pair to dare to jump in front of your forefather,' Gabriel comments. 'Now we all know he's going to come for her and that's why the Militant is doing his bit, but it won't hold him long. You,' he points to me, 'come with me.'

I follow Gabriel out and downstairs into the grounds. We walk in an uneasy silence as we make our way to the centre piece of the garden. The fountain with the statue I truly hate. It represents so much and Gabriel is making a point, because we stop there and he looks at it for a moment before speaking.

I wonder what his feelings are? That statue means a lot to him too. Part of his story. No matter my feelings, he is my elder and lost just as much. He's fighting every instinct when it comes to Mina in order to do the right thing. Last time, he'd tried and failed again. Even if she wasn't the real Primum. He still loved her. He still loved the boy and watched Sebastian bring him up as his own.

'Do you think that is a likeness?' Gabriel suddenly says.

I wasn't made at that time, Master,' I answer honestly.

'But you see Mina in her face?' he pushes.

Of course I see Mina in her face. She's a pure double and the only reason I didn't see it before is because I didn't want to. The Primum then is not like Mina now. She was unpredictable, easily led and wanted more than the Powers were willing to give. Nothing like Mina. Well the Mina before the change.

'All Marleys share the same look,' I answer.

Gabriel turns my way with a look of annoyance.

'Your precious Deanna didn't look like her though.'

I bristle at his comment. I want to fight for her honour, but if she'd have been the Primum then I wouldn't have been able to love her.

'I apologise,' Gabriel offers. 'Deanna was special and I did feel for her, but she wasn't the one. She wasn't Mina. You have to admit that.'

'I do know that. I've seen it every day since she were born and watched her own mother struggle with knowing the same thing. But when will it end Gabriel? When will the Marleys be free?' I ask.

'Do you think I like this? If Marleux hadn't have raped the girl then none of this would have happened. Sebastian as he's called now would have had what was his and blah blah.'

'That's true,' I say. 'But you...'

'Go on?'

I turn away from Gabriel's glare. Its' still raw for him even after all this time. Yes Marleux's actions are at the root of Mina's problems, but what Gabriel failed to do is just as bad, because the three of them are all entwined in all this crap.

'Well there's no denying that Mina and Sebastian are now together, maybe there's a way I can make this deal end with Mina.'

'You would do that?' I ask.

Gabriel now looks me in the eye and I see sadness and a little defeat there.

'I feel the connection just as Sebastian does. When I first laid eyes on her in the hospital bed, I loved her all over again, but I can't have her and if she's to be happy then I will allow her to be with Sebastian.'

'And what if she still loves Micka?' I dare ask.

'I will do everything in my power to stop them being together. I will not allow another angel to make my mistakes.'

And there it is. The real Gabriel behind the arrogance. The one that cares for his fellow angels. So it wasn't jealousy, but not wanting Micka to be caught up in this Marley legacy. No doubt though the Powers cannot afford for someone like Micka to be indisposed. He's too strong and too important to the Militants.

'What will we do about Marleux?' I ask.

'He only wants her because she is almost giving in to her succubus nature. If we can get her back to the Mina we all know then he will leave us alone. He's trying to prove a point. It's the Emandato that is our real problem.'

'How close are they?' I ask.

'Close enough. I just wish I knew which angel was leading them,' he mutters.

When we return to the Manor, Sebastian is laid beside Mina. She's still unconscious and seems to be still and peaceful. Sebastian's arms are holding on for dear life and a look of pain passes across Gabriel's face. Then Micka enters the room and it passes through Gabriel to Micka. My daughter has truly got these men under her charm and the three of them are going to have to work together to get her through this.

'Have you sealed the Manor down, Militant?' Gabriel asks.

'As much as I possibly can, Master,' Micka bows.

'Uzrel?'

'Yes, Master.'

Uzrel steps forward expectantly.

'Take Miss Marley from this place and into the Marley basement.'

'What?!' I shout.

'If you want her to go back to what she was then she needs to go to where Marleux was summoned,' Gabriel snaps.

'But Marleux...'

'Will go to her and kill two birds with one stone,' Gabriel finishes.

Sebastian pulls himself from the bed.

'Then I will go with her,' he says.

'No, Uzrel is the only one who can take her.' Gabriel turns to Uzrel and pulls him to one side. 'I'm trusting you will be able to keep her at bay. You will need to prove yourself as her guardian.'

Uzrel nods and going to the bed picks her up and disappears leaving Sebastian to cuss.

With Uzrel with Mina, there is nothing much we can do but wait. Wait and see if the Emandato show up. But first we need to call on the town to help us.

Ray's Journal cont...

Of course the town is on-board to help me. Everyone loves Mina. She is one of their own, but there is a fear amongst them. They are scared of the Emandato and Marleux. The former hasn't set foot in this town since its birth, but his reputation is enough to get people prickly. But there is one person missing and I have no choice but to go see her myself. Beg her to forgive and forget.

So here I am standing in Jaq's small bedroom feeling awkward and invasive. My second daughter looks up at me all defensive and tells me that she no longer what's anything to do with Mina. She's got Candice now. But I have to make her understand that yes, Candice has a role to play, but the bond that she and Mina have formed is greater and right now Mina needs her. But Jaq is no fool and won't just accept my word so I tell her everything and I mean everything. Who Mina is—the lot.

The poor girl sits on her bed and stares up at me with wide eyes and a pale face. I realise that what I've always known is a big thing for those that know and love Mina. To know that she was a succubus was no great surprise to most of us, those of us who were old enough to keep it secret, because they knew Daniel and Deanna, but to know that Mina is a Primum and what that means to the world is a lot to get your head around.

'Does she know any of this?' Jaq asks and I shake my head.

'You can't tell her either. You only know because I need your help. Supton has to pull together.'

'So all this bullshit that she's turned into is all part of the change?' Jaq asks.

'Yes, the Mina we know and love is still there deep down and now we have to get her back.'

It takes only a few hours for us to get word that Marleux has arrived in town, but what we need is the Emandato to come too. But Marleux is better than nothing.

We find him in Mina's, perched on one of the stools at the counter. The place is closed thanks to our earlier warning. Daniel and I go to try and reason with him. If the Emandato come then we need him onside while also stabbing him in the back. Something we are getting far too good at this place.

'Your son is one clever bastard,' Marleux sneers.

'Yes,' Daniel says.

Marleux spins in his seat so he now faces us.

'I like him,' he says to us. 'He's a strong pull too. It's a shame he didn't get to Mina first. A pure born would have been prefect.'

'We'd never let that happen?' I snap.

Marleux looks my way and his lips curl in disgust.

'I'd call you a fallen angel, but only one person is worth that title. You are just a fuck up.'

'A fuck up who gave the world its Primum,' I add.

'It seems the fall gave you a pair, angel. Anyway, I'm not a total bastard. I want to know why you called.'

Daniel and I glance at each other. Could he be being reasonable?

'The Emandato is wanting Mina dead and with her in the state she's in it makes her vulnerable. I wanted you to help get her back,' I say.

'Why would I do that?'

'Because you're...'

'Because I'm their forefather? Do I look like the man upstairs? I fucked the prize virgin and that's all I did. I didn't expect a bloodline,' Marleux says.

'But you're position in hell, Father?' Daniel asks.

'Yes, I suppose I am now better than those fucking Robrattos. Fine!' Marleux sighs. 'I will help, but I am not doing it without a price and I want to know where she is.'

'What's the price?'

Is all I get out, before the window of Mina's is smashed in. Turning, we see an old face. One we thought was gone. The Roberts girl, Laura and another older man, whom I assume is her father. Marleux moves from the stool and I hear him hiss a name.

I was wrong. By Marleux's cuss, that is not Laura's father. That is Robratto. That father demon of the Roberts. I've only ever heard of the demon, but not seen him and I realise how much alike the two of them are. Both small in stature and dark in colouring and I don't trust neither of them. Daniel is out of the window, before I can stop him, but Robratto soon has him on the floor.

'Where is she?' Robratto shouts.

'Well well well, who dragged you from the pit?' Marleux says stepping through the broken window.

'I, unlike some have no need to be near that place. I've better things to be doing like taking care of my bloodline,' Robratto answers.

'She is one of yours?' Marleux asks.

'Laura, meet the original Marley. See what is claimed to be so great.'

The power pull between the incubi is strong and it's not just coming from the old ones, but with Daniel and Laura too. The electric pulse of sexual energy bouncing off one another and trying to dominate. The air is rippling with it, so much so my body pulsates almost like it did when I had the powers of an angel.

'I see what you mean,' Laura says.

'Don't mock, Miss Roberts, my niece soon drove you out of town, Daniel throws.

'She cheated,' Laura snaps.

'She's a succubus, Girl,' Marleux mocks.

'Enough chit chat, where is this special Marley then?' Robratto asks.

'Why do you want to know?' I ask pushing forward slightly.

I may be the only human in the group now I've no wings, but it doesn't mean I'm weak either.

'The halfbreed's father I take it,' Robratto asks Laura, who nods. 'Well, you must know by now that we are working with the Emandato who have kindly offered us a good price for the head of the half-breed.'

'Which is?' Marleux asks.

'If we kill your girl then mine can take her place and the Marleys will be over.'

'You son of a bitch,' Daniel hisses.

'Incubus,' Robratto throws back.

'She's somewhere where neither of you can find her,' I say.

'We'll see.'

'What the...' Laura exclaims.

We all look around us and I see the whole town is in force. Those that are Weres have changed. The Shifters to whatever beast they can and there are the Faes led by Candice. My insides swell with pride at the sight. As a town we have our problems, but when it comes to each other, we pull together.

'If you want Mina, you'll have to come through us first?' Candice announces.

'It's a little overkill for just two little demons,' Robratto sneers.

Candice moves forward and I catch a glimpse of Christine in her face. She means business and that fills me comfort.

'In this town there's no such thing as overkill,' she says. 'Now kindly leave or you'll find out just what this town can do.'

Laura grabs at Robratto's arm nervously. She remembers what happened when they thought she'd attacked Mina.

'We are not leaving so do your worst.'

Suddenly, my phone rings and pulling it from pocket I answer the withheld number. I hear only one sentence before suddenly finding myself back my home.

'What the fuck?' Daniel exclaims.

Gabriel and Sebastian run towards us. There is pure panic in their faces. This isn't good.

'The demons were a diversion. The Emandato has sent someone to the Manor. They know she's not there.'

'Is Uzrel still with Mina?' I ask.

'Still locked in the cellar. Jono has put the enchantment up. Whoever goes through that door goes to hell,' Sebastian adds.

'What's the plan?' I demand.

'We give them what they want,' Gabriel says.

'Fuck that!'

'No way.'

'You will not.'

'You will have to go through me first.'

We all say together.

Gabriel raises his hands at us.

'Calm yourselves. You all have places to be and I need you all to trust me. Uzrel is with her safely guarded, but we need them to go to the pits.'

We listen carefully to Gabriel's plan and despite our reservation it is a good plan and we know it will work. I ask how Uzrel is coping with Mina in a locked room and he informs me that Uzrel is holding up very well. I have no choice but to hand over all my trust and power to the one angel who I trust the least with my daughter and wait for the Emandato to make their move, and boy did they make their move.

#

Tannini's Journal 30th May 2330hrs

When Williamina Francs cast the chaos spell on Supton in order to kidnap Mina I thought I saw the town at its worst. Now I've seen the town at its best. Everyone's exhausted, but we stood strong and I'm fucking proud.

We had gathered in the town centre near Mina's and I mean the whole fucking town all in whatever guise they felt powerful. Candice was leading us to make a stand. I stood with Beverley at my side and was shocked at seeing the father of the Marleys standing with my good friend. I mean that dirty fucker is part of mythology and yet there he was looking no more special than any other fucking demon. But I could feel the power coming from their direction. I'd considered changing, but I felt happier as a man than animal.

It all seemed so simple. Show the Incubi the power we had as a town and push them out, but then Ray and Danny were zapped out of there by one of the angels, leaving Marleux and Robratto shocked. We all looked at each other a little speechless. Then Robratto and Laura also disappeared.

'What the fuck is going on?' Marleux shouted. 'Fae, come here.'

Everyone looked at Candice and started to take a step back from her and she gives a look of exasperation.

'I said Fae, come here,' he snaps again.

'No,' Candice shouts back. 'Fuck off.'

With a click of his fingers, Candice is in his hands and I feel my body want to shift, but Beverley catches my eye and shakes her head slowly.

'When I tell you to do something, you do it,' Marleux snaps. 'Now, I want you to trace the Roberattos.'

'And why would I help you?' she croaks.

Marleux releases her and I expect Candice to run back to us, but she does something better and punches him in the face. He barely flinches, but it shows balls.

'I like you Fae. I like you a lot,' he says. 'If I tell you that Mina is in danger and I can save her will that help?'

Candice seems to ponder on this for a moment, before she asks what she needs to do.

'I need you to get something that Mina really loves.'

Candice smiled at him. 'I've just the thing.

Mina and Marleux

Candice's Journal 31st May 2245hrs

Having that demon's hands around my neck was the scariest thing that I've ever encountered. The smell of him was intense and seemed to invade my body. Sulphuric is one way to describe it, but that's too obvious. If you tried to think of the most toxic smell that could invade your body and soul and times it by 100 then that's what Marleux smelt of.

Lorreli says to me: 'If there's a good time for you not to be you then this is it.'

But I couldn't. I am me. I'm Candice Rose. I'm cut from the same loaf as Christine and fuck me, my barbed tongue gets me some respect.

'I like you,' he states.

But using Mina, he knew I'd help him. He told me that he needed something that she loved and so I took him back to my house. He was pleasant and polite as he stood in my space and I couldn't help, but relax in his presence.

'You should have taken Tannini with you,' Lorreli chastised.

'Because I've got this. Trust me, I whispered.

'So, you were born on the same day as Mina?' he said.

'Apparently,' I shouted as I grabbed what I needed from upstairs.

'Do you know how you are connected?' he said as I entered the front room.

'I've been made aware of some of it. I know what it means that Mina is the Primum, what I am to her, I've no idea. Here, this will help.'

'What on earth is this piece of crap?'

Marleux's lips curled in disgust at the plaid shirt of Micka's

'You wanted something that Mina loved and the owner of that shirt is just that.'

Marleux looks again at it.

'This is Sebastian Daniels?'

I looked at him shocked. How could he not know? Is hell really that closed off?

'Mina is engaged to Sebastian, but her heart belongs to Micka. The Militant.'

Suddenly the front door crashed open.

'Leave my cousin alone you messed up fucker.'

Well that's new. Jaq sticking up for me and standing up against Marleux.

#

Ray's Journal 31st May 2230hrs

The Emandato must be really desperate. No change that, they are desperate. They have sent a very powerful Fae. One that even I know about.

Christine used to talk about her with a little fear. I always worried about Candice, but she was just a dabbler. This Fae is the real deal. Her name is Tyia. She is like Christine and a Fae with magick power.

All Faes have some ability to play with magick, such as glamour and spell work. Small stuff really. There were born from Canaan, an angel. Whereas there are a small number who are incredibly powerful and it's rumoured that they have the blood of the Great Mother in them, but who knows. But where Christine used hers for good, Tyia is all for the darkside so to speak. She was waiting for us all at Manor, where she had already broken the magick that protects the place.

Of course Mina is not there and Gabriel had brought Sebastian to us and then brought us to them.

Now Gabriel tells us his plan to bring them all to Mina, both Daniel and I protest. But of course he's right. I know what he's planning will work, but the father in me wants to keep them as far away from my daughter has possible.

'Where's Micka?' I ask.

'He's at the Manor,' Sebastian answers.

'Well if he dies it will solve your little problem,' Daniel says.

'He's the strongest we have,' Sebastian throws. 'I don't feel threatened by Micka.'

'Sure you don't.'

'Boys, calm down,' Gabriel snaps. 'The Fae wytch will be nothing to the Militant. He's just delaying her. No one dies today on my watch unless I want them to.'

The look on his face causes me to believe. He may be up his own arse, but Gabriel is a man of his word and that is no lie.

Then my phone rings and it's Tannini. He tells me that Marleux has taken Candice. I know what this means, but I'm scared that Candice has no idea what she's taken on.

'What's happening?' Daniel asks.

'Marleux is getting Candice to help him.'

Gabriel turns my way.

'Is that the Rose girl? Christine's granddaughter?'

'Yes, she's Mina's other half,' I answer.

'For fucks sake,' Gabriel cusses.

'It looks like the town is making it's a way to us too,' Daniel points out.

Looking out of the window, we all see the Supton's residents making their way to me.

'Good that's what we need,' Gabriel say. 'They will lead the way. Where's Jonathan, I have another idea.'

The Dark Wytch

Candice's Journal 1st June 2230hrs

Seeing Jaq standing up for me is shock enough for me to be silenced almost. But Marleux just looks amused at her attempt at bravado.

'And what you going to do little girl?' he asks.

'I'm a Rose,' Jaq answers.

'And…?'

'Jaq, it's fine,' I say stepping between them.

'So where were we—yes, this shitty shirt is the Militant's, and Mina…?'

'Mina maybe engaged to Sebastian, but her heart belongs to Micka and don't even ask why she's with Sebastian, cause we don't even get it. Anyway, that's his so use it,' I say.

'What in hell are you doing giving him that?' Jaq turns on me. 'I fucking knew you'd stab her in the back. You're a fucking joke.'

'Jaq, you need to fucking back off,' I snap.

'You know Mina thinks a lot of you and I've no idea why?'

That's a surprise. I thought Mina just put up with me because of Lorreli. I've no words, but she continues to name call me. All the anger and resentment since Nanna brimming to the surface, and so does my own anger. Before I know what's happening, we are both wrestling on the floor. I hadn't realised she knew how to fight and that surprise causes her to get the upper hand.

I've been in some fights in my time, ones where I've had to fight for my life or get out of some shit I'd got myself into, but Jaq is showing her gall as a Rose and has me on the floor. I feel every bit of resentment and hatred aimed towards me. Yet, she holds back. She could pummel me to the ground, but doesn't. This cousin of mine cares and that's a shock too.

Suddenly a pair of hands grabs us both easily and lifts us to our feet.

'Ladies, please. As much as a turn on this is, I need the Fae with the power to take me to Mina and save her from the Emandato.'

We both look at Marleux and apologise.

'Now, Candice is it? I need you with me, Jaq, you can go back to Ray and tell him my intentions.'

'Which are?' she asks.

Marleux touches Jaq's cheek and not only do I hear my sap cousin sigh, but almost melt. For fucks sake what is it about my cousin and these Marleys.

'No more questions pretty one. Just do it.'

And fuck me off she skips.

'Now, you, are you ready?' he asks me.

'For what?'

'This Militant will be protecting Mina and this will take me right to her.'

He grabs me by the waist and pulls me close. I want to recoil, but can't. The pull he has *is* strong. Hard to resist no matter what he looks like. No wonder he's the greatest incubus in hell.

Before I know it, we are both in the grounds of the fucking Manor and all hell is breaking loose. The power I feel ripples through me and it's not feeling good. Whatever's here is big and dark.

Taking my arm, Marleux drags me towards the house and there we see a group of around twenty people all trying to smash their way into the Manor. There's a mixture of beings from all walks of life, even some human and whatever magick is protecting the Manor it's holding strong.

'The Emandato,' we both say together.

'Why is this place so protected?' I ask.

Marleux looks at me as though I'm stupid.

'Because this is where it all began. This is where the Marley story begins.'

'Where you raped that girl?'

Marleux doesn't answer, but instead marches towards where the group are now looking our way.

'Don't mind us,' he says calmly.

How can he be so calm? I'm shitting myself, however, not one being comes toward us. There's a lot to be said about the power of demonic strut.

Then that power I felt gets stronger and with it pure black hatred. Something I fucking thought I knew, but nothing compared to this. I look up at what's coming towards us, dressed in a little flowery dress and it is a Fae I think I recognise, or believe I should. Her hair is bright blond and long and curly. Very pretty, girly pretty. Like Jaq. But that's the only resemblance. She's evil and fucked up.

'You must be a Rose,' she says. 'And you...who are you?'

Marleux doesn't answer, but grabs my arm and pulls me towards the Manor.

'Not so fast demon.'

A flash hits and floors us both. My whole body feels like it's on fire, then I'm being pulled to my feet by the hair.

'You didn't answer my question?' she hisses.

'It sounded more like a statement than a question,' I answer trying to squirm my way from her grasp.

'With a smart mouth like that you are Christine's granddaughter.'

'Then you'll know that you shouldn't mess with a Rose,' I say.

'Faes, ladies, come on there's no need to fight. It seems we all want the same thing,' Marleux steps in. 'No matter how sexy it may end up becoming.'

'What's it to you…wait, are you a Marley?'

'I am THE Marley and you are in my way and I don't give a fuck who you are,' he answers. 'Now give me the Fae and let me carry on.'

'You'll be lucky to get inside. There's some angel in there holding me out.'

'I've just told you I am THE Marley. I can walk anywhere in this town.'

My hair is released and Marleux has her attention as she sidles up to him like a whore on heat. This bitch is good.

'So then you will help me get past the angel,' she purrs.

'You've enough power to take him down,' Marleux answers. 'Why do you need me?'

'I don't, but having a Marley onside will help our cause.'

He catches my eye briefly and understand fully what he wants me to do. I throw all the dark magic I have towards her, but fuck me, she fires it all back. Thanks to Lorreli, it only knocks me off my feet. Tyia's attention is back on me and she's pissed.

Her minions have us surrounded and one of them has the fucking mordacity to lay their hands on me. He's a Were. I can smell the beast on him and it turns my stomach. He gives me a low growl as I fight against him.

'Be still bitch.'

'That's funny, it's something I'd call your mother,' I throw.

Turning me around, he strikes me across the face and the start of a curse emerges from my lips. I'll make the son of a bitch pay, but Lorreli stops me with a warning not to be so brash and save my power for the real fight.

'You touch her again and I will strike you down myself,' Tyia snaps.

'She called my ma,' he growls.

'She's a Rose and deserves respect.' Then she turns towards me with a smile. 'I have heard a lot about you. You've a real talent for the dark arts.'

'I know my shit,' I answer.

'You clearly do. So why are you here fighting for a town that don't care about you. Stand at my side and we can show them all that the Fae is at the top of the power chain.'

'Above the angels? You really are delusion.'

'We are derived from angels. It's what our Great Mother would want.'

As she moves closer to me, my skin prickles with the circling of power between us. Her comment about our Great Mother has fucking bristled me and its damn hard keeping your cool, when nature tells you to put them on their arse.

'Gabriel doesn't believe she will come back,' I answer.

Tyia takes a small step back and looks a little bit pale.

'Gabriel is here?'

'Yes,' I nod. 'He's protecting the Marley girl. Surely, you'd know that.'

'What about you?' she asks turning towards Marleux.

'What about me, sweetheart?'

'Are you on the side of the angels?'

Marleux bellows out a laugh that startles us both.

'The side of the angel? Sweetheart, do I look like I do business with angels?'

'Then welcome to the fold,' she says.

Again Marleux laughs. Can he really that easily amused? Hell can't be that much of bad place if his spirits are that high.

'My dear child, I am not fighting on your side either. I have no care about what fight you're fighting. I just want to get into my home.'

'This belongs to Mr Daniels and I want the same thing,' she answers.

I can't fucking believe what I'm seeing. This Fae is trying to seduce the king of seduction. She flirts around him, slightly touching his body with her own. Marleux doesn't seem to care. He's probably seen it all before.

'This, sweetheart, is a Marley property. Mr Daniels is just a lodger.'

'Maybe, once we get in to the house you and I can create a better bloodline than the last one.'

His reactions are lightning fast and causes me to step back. But no one is as surprised as Tyia who now wears his hand mark across her cheek. Strangely enough, not one of her minions moves to her defence. That is interesting.

'I only fuck with the pure,' he hisses.

Darkness leaves her fingers towards Marleux and it knocks him clean off his feet. She is seriously pissed off and she's just getting started. Standing over him, murmuring words that make me shudder, he's now writhing on the ground in pain.

Lorreli, I really need you to talk me through this.

'Then trust me,' is all I hear before I'm suddenly at Micka's side. He looks beyond stressed. This Fae must have really been testing him.

'Where did you come from?' he asks, shocked.

'I came here with Marleux,' I answer.

'You did what?' he shouts. 'I've got enough on keeping this Tyia out of this place.'

'He wants to help us?'

'And why would he do that and what can he do that I can't?'

'He says he can bring her back. Anyway, why are you struggling? I thought you could kill anything?'

He gives me a dark look and all I can do is shrug. It's a simple question.

'I can kill anything, but the highest order of angels and the Powers. That Fae out there is protected by some serious angel power and I can't break her.'

'She's only a Fae. I could try something.'

Micka starts to smile as something suddenly occurs to him and I suddenly feel nervous.

'Tell Micka, I know what he's thinking.'

Lorreli's voice makes me fucking jump.

Why what's he thinking? I ask her.

'Do you trust us both?' she asks.

Stop fucking about and just tell me

I flinch at the touch of Micka's hand on my arm.

'I understand if you say no, but it's the only way.'

'I'm not an angel,' I say.

'I need to be inside you,' he says and I nearly choke out.

'Yeah and so do most guys,' I splutter back.

'Candice, you know what I mean. Lorreli and I need to switch places and in your body will be the power of a Miltiant and a Rose.'

'You're right, the answer is no. I'm not letting Lorreli go just to let you in.'

The thought of letting go of Lorreli makes me shit scared never mind having to cope with Micka inside my head and to take on this Tyia. I'm going to get killed.

'Calm down, Candice. Micka would not put you in any danger if he didn't think you could handle it. You know you are powerful and you've practised the dark part of magick. Go there and with Micka inside you than you will be as strong as Mina,' Lorreli says.

Then why can't you do it?

'Because, I'm not as equipped as Micka. I can't do what he does.'

'For fucks sake,' I curse. 'Fine, what do I need to do?'

Micka smiles. 'I need you to sing.'

'You need me to what? You know what I don't want to know. Fine! Let's get this over with.'

And I start to sing some nursery rhyme that Nanna used to sing to me. I hear Micka tell me to keep singing and then suddenly, my body feels like it's about to be ripped in two as Lorreli leaves and Micka enters. I know the exact moment he's in, because every feeling he has for Mina floods my system. Pure love, confusion, jealousy and so much pain and anger.

Jesus, he really did love that angelicdemon

'You need to turn off some of that emotion big guy, I can't breathe in here.'

Micka apologises, but only switches down a notch.

'Use everything I've got. I know you've learned to control all your anger and that's good, but right now I need you to find it and use it and take that bitch down together.'

'And what about Marleux?'

'If he can bring Mina back than I will let him live.'

Tannini's Journal 1st June 2230hrs

I don't know who decided that it was a good idea for us all to be at Ray's but that's where we ended up. All that was missing were the pitchforks and I'd find the whole fucking thing funny if it weren't for Mina being in trouble.

Marleux has taken Candice to wherever, no doubt to seduce her into doing his bidding. I just hope that little dark Fae proves her worth.

As we near the house, Jono comes out and greets us and he tells us Gabriel's plan. I already know what Jono can do and how it works, but I'm not sure that we as a town can pull off that sort of magick and deception. But when he tells me who the Emandato have sent, then anything is better than nothing.

I've heard of Tyia McMann and she is one messed up son of a bitch. I came across her once in my entire career. One of my human colleagues brought her in for some assault charge. She'd attacked and beat a few beefy guys in a bar. We were all in for a shock when he brought it this petite little woman in a pretty little dress. She looked like you could blow her over. I knew better of course. I could smell the darkness all around her. She of course used her magick to break out and the duty officer suffered a major breakdown after. The poor guy.

Using a trick, that Danny had learned, Jono covered the whole town with the Marley scent by chanting some spell. Poor Jono had to perform his mojo with most of the town watching him. He should be used to an audience given his new found fame, but this isn't singing or playing a guitar, this is magick that he knows very little about. It took Danny to join him for it to work. Both Marley men muttering their magick and giving us some of that power. It fell on us like a mist and stuck to hair, skin and clothes. It's strange. There was no smell, but there is a hint of a scent and my inner animal wants to repel it.

'It's not too much for you all to start...you know,' Jono mutters. 'But it will confuse Tyia enough that we can get her away from the Manor to us and with her, she'll bring Marleux.'

'I don't get it. Why didn't you just get her here in the first place?' I asked.

'Because, we are hoping that Micka can weaken her and that way the trap will be easier to set.'

So that's what happened and the events that unfolded was something that will stay with me for the rest of my life.

Candice's Journal cont...

As soon as Micka enters my body then the hold he has over the Manor comes crashing down and there in the doorway is Tyia. I barely get my mouth open when I'm hit by something that makes my body sting. Whatever it is it makes me writhe on the floor and I can't seem to break it. She grabs me by the hair and pulls me to her face.

'I'm done messing bitch, where is the Primum?'

'Why didn't you ask Marleux?' I manage.

With a click of her fingers one of her minions drags in the limp body of Marleux and vomit starts to churn in the back of my throat. How the fuck did she manage to take down an old demon like that? And why didn't he fight back? The answer must be that she's too good. Micka senses my fear and I hear him tell me not to worry. Just use him.

'It's taken her a lot of power to do this, she's getting weaker, but has no idea,' he says.

How can she have no idea?

'Because she's drunk on power and that makes her stupid,' Micka answers.

'Now Rose, where is my prize?'

Lorreli in Micka's body makes a move towards her, but not being used to it causes her to stumble awkwardly and Tyia laughs fuelling my own anger.

'Good, focus on that,' Micka says. 'Soon, we are going to hit her with all we've got. Now look down at the floor.'

I subtly direct my gaze to the floor and I see that Marleux is wearing the smallest of smirks that I was sure wasn't there before. Fuck me, he's playing dead.

Then I realise why he's smiling, there's the sound of music coming from outside, and singing. What the fuck? Who the fuck is singing? Then I get my answer as my body starts to respond in every way. It's like being hit by a wave of endorphins and it feels good. Tyia's grip loosens as she turns towards the open door and we both see most of the town coming down the large drive.

'Keep your head,' Micka warns 'Don't fall for the Marley charm.'

I will try

'What is going on,' Tyia asks finally letting me go.

I don't know why, but I can tell she's getting weaker. She's used far too much power to get as far as she has and to try and fight the Marley charm will deplete her further.

'I feel funny,' she complains.

'That's because you are fighting a Marley.'

She jumps as Marleux gets to his feet.

'You were dead,' she splutters.

'I'm the King of all Incubi, I don't die.'

'Get ready,' Micka warns.

Fury consumes her as her minions walk like zombies toward where the town are coming towards us. As those that can turn do, the place erupts into a brawl as town fight minion. This is going to get fucked up. Is the angelicdemon really that important? The thought causes Micka to tense inside me. Shit! I forgot he was in there.

Tyia doesn't know where to aim first. This new development is messing with her head and more importantly draining her.

'You fucking arsehole,' she screams as electric blue light erupts from her fingers towards Marleux. We all flinch, but the magick splutters before it hits its target. She starts to scream and Marleux gives me a nod like he knows what we are about to do just as Micka screams *Now!!* in my head.

The three of us cling together as we are transported to some basement and it isn't until I see Mina and Uz that I realise what we've done. Both Tyia and Marleux throw themselves towards Mina and to my surprise Uz does nothing. I start to move forward, but Micka holds me to the spot and I mean holds me. I'm immobilised like a statue.

What the fuck are you doing? That's your girlfriend

'I'm stopping you from being stupid and Mina will never be my girlfriend, so don't refer to her that way.'

So stuck in some frozen spell all I can do is watch what unfolds. Mina is like an animal, eager to embrace them and as they run towards her, she jumps from the bed and with a growl punches the plaster of the ceiling. It's then that I fucking see it. The magick seal and so do Marleux and Tyia, but it's too late as a swirling vortex opens up beneath them and with a shrug, Marleux falls into it. But Tyia is not going without a fight.

She goes to grab at Mina, who is hanging from the ceiling beam, but only just. I feel Micka tense up inside me. He knows he's trapped and can't help without putting me in danger. This is new I feel fucking bad. He can save her, but I'm stopping him.

Luckily, Uzrel throws some of his own power her way to try and knock down the hole, but Mina, hanging just within reach is still in his range and it's too damn close. Power bounces off the walls from both Tyia fighting for her life and Uzrel trying to save Mina. The noise is deafening and all I want to do is cower in the corner.

I've considered what hell must feel like, but the power and energy coming from the vortex pulls at every dark power that sits within me. My body is convulsing from the inside out. It isn't helping that I have an angel in there. Good and evil fighting for space. Is this what Mina feels like? That girl deserves some of my respect.

Then, Mina's eyes meet mine and I know damn well she's not seeing me. She knows who's inside my body, especially when Micka, using my voice shouts: 'Don't you dare.'

That stupid idiot, she lets go and not only am I blinded by so much light and noise, but it's like the whole world is crashing down around me. I must have blacked out, because when I awake I'm back in my own bed with my family around me. Jaq is sitting on my bed sobbing really hard and no one will look me in the eye.

'Why are you all here? Where's Mina?' I ask.

Then they tell me what happened when Mina let go and what happened to me. Who saved my life and why no one will look me in the eye. I stumble from the bed and make it to bathroom just in time to vomit. This whole town is going to hate me. Mina is going to hate me. Why did he save me?

Sacrifice

Tannini's Journal 5th of June 2245hrs.

I'm writing this after leaving Beverley in bed. I just can't rest. The whole thing keeps going through my head and no matter what scenero I try and come up with to fix it, I can't. No one can. And Mina—poor poor Mina. How could she lose him like that? How could he have been so stupid?

We were all stood outside where Mina was locked in. Waiting for Candice to do her thing and bring Tyia and Marleux. Most of the town had gone to the Manor covered in the Marley scent, singing. I was going to join them, but Ray had asked me to stay with him and Danny. With Sebastian pacing, the whole place was beyond tense anyway and I think he needed someone steady with him. I hated leaving Beverley, but she told me to stay.

Gabriel was constantly at the door, trying to talk Uzrel. I could tell by the pace that Gabriel was talking that Mina was causing her guardian angel a lot of problems. All I could hear was Gabriel telling him to keep calm and to focus on what he was trying to do. I think Gabriel was doing his own little mojo to try and ease Uzrel's pain. Whispering words of encouragement and some angel chant.

'Marleux is coming,' Danny said suddenly.

'How?'

Was all I get out when practically all hell broke loose in the literal sense. We could hear the sound of something like a tornado behind the door and Uzrel shouting.

'What if she gets sucked into hell,' Ray screamed at Gabriel.

'Then I go in and I drag her back out. Trust me, she will survive this,' Gabriel reassured.

But Ray was not having any of it and that's when it all became fucked up.

Micka shouting something and then, as Ray reached for the door, a flash of electric blue light burst through the wood knocking us all off our feet.

The noise was deafening and I managed to see Mina disappear into the swirling vortex into hell with Tyia holding her. Danny and Sebastian was screaming, running towards the hole, but Gabriel held them back. For what seemed like hours later, but really only seconds, Marleux was crawling his way back out and with a salute, threw Mina back out towards us where she landed like a ragdoll, before falling back where he came from.

'The son of bitch saved her,' Danny gasped as he ran towards where Mina struggled to get up from the floor. She reached out for Sebastian, but said Micka's name and I saw both Candice and Sebastian flinch. It's then I understand why I heard Micka voice's. He'd taken control of that poor Fae.

But something was wrong. The one person who should have been first to Mina was not there. I turned to find out where he was and the sight brought me to my knees. With a burning hole in his chest, motionless on the floor is my best friend.

It's like the whole place freeze framed breaking only when Mina started screaming. We all tried to save him. Dr Powell came as fast as he could, but nothing. Mina begged for Gabriel or Uzrel to heal him, but they told her that it was impossible he'd already gone.

Sebastian picked up Mina and with Gabriel, disappeared no doubt back to the Manor. If it was at all possible I could still hear her scream and then Candice disappeared.

I helped Dr Powell to wrap my best friend's body and with Danny, we put him in the back of the ambulance. Soon the whole town was at the gate watching and tears streaming down each of their faces. Then, Jono pushed through the crowd and looked stricken. Danny had to drag him away. The Marleys had lost one of their own in order to try and save the Primum. The problem is is that the Primum will never forgive herself.

Looking out my bedroom window, the night is unusually still and I'm not sure what will happen tomorrow. Hearing, movement behind, I feel Beverley's arms wrap around my waist from behind.

'Baby, you need to get some sleep,' she whispers.

'How can I sleep after everything that happened?'

She moves around so now I'm looking at her. Worry and tiredness is all over her face and I don't know how I can change that.

'What if we run?' she asks.

I shrug even as she pulls off her nightshirt and changes in front of me into dog. Her brown eyes looking up at me. May she is right. Maybe I just need to run it off.

Jaq's Email to Carla 6th June 1030hrs

Hon,

I don't know what else to say. First Nanna and now Ray. This town is dropping like flies and no one is able to stop it. This used to be a great place to live and now it's like the grim reaper is hanging around every little corner to take who he can.

All I want to do is see Mina and make sure she's alright, but no one is letting us in. Sebastian has got her on clampdown and I've no idea what's going on. Mum and Dad have both gone to Candice's to speak to her.

I've no idea why no one will speak to me. I'm not a child any longer. It's not just Candice. I have my own problems, but no one wants to hear about that.

No one wants to hear that I've missed my period and I'm shitting myself that I could be carrying the next generation of a Marley. I daren't even do a test, because I don't want to know the result.

To have Jono's baby was always a dream of mine, but not this way. Not when I am with Dom and that was also before I knew what it meant to be a Marley. What if I have a girl? Will it be just like Mina?

I know you're going to think I'm jumping the gun and that stress of the past few weeks have not helped, but I can't help being scared. I just wish I could talk to Mina.

Mina's Online Journal 6th June 1945hrs

I'm done with the lot of them. Every angel could fall flat dead on this planet for all I care. Not one of them, who claim that they loved me, lifted a finger to save my dad. They all just stood there and allowed him to die. I know they could have healed him if they wanted to, but what it all boiled down to is that he's no longer one of them. He'd done his duty and it's over.

Sebastian keeps checking on me, but I don't even want him near. I just want to be alone. He even dared to ask me if I remembered about hell. I practically screamed in his face.

In all honesty, I don't remember much but being cold and the feeling of desolation. The cold was the most unsettling, I always thought as much of you have done that Hell is a hot place of sulphur and lava and maybe it is, but as far as I got it was just icy cold. It was the helplessness as I fell that was scary. I was ready to go where ever. I didn't care, but I couldn't deal with feeling helpless and out of control.

My thoughts turned to everyone I love. My father, Jono, Micka and Sebastian. Would they miss me now I'm gone. Maybe Micka or even Gabriel will come for me?

No! no angel will ever cross the border to that. Hell only houses one angel and that's enough. Closing my eyes, I'm ready for whatever pit I fall into. Until Marleux grabbed hold. Wrapping his arms around me, he made me look him in the eye.

'You read that damned book?' he shouted over the noise, the hole created and I nodded.

'Then you know who you are and why Sebastian?'

Again I nod.

'Yet your heart belongs to the angel?'

'I can't help it.'

'Gabriel is liar. The future he showed you was a false one. He needed…we needed you to be with Sebastian and now you know why.'

'Because Gabriel and you stole me from him?'

Marleux looked at me puzzled.

'You read the book?'

'Yes, but not all of it. I just saw that I am the Primum and what you did.'

Marleux held me tighter to him, worry crossed his face.

'You will always be the princess of both worlds, honour them both and they will bend to your will. One day you're going to need them to. Now let's get you the fuck out of here.'

'Why would you save me?'

'Because you are my blood and despite how much I fucking hate it. I will always be loyal to my own. Just make sure you keep it a secret, I have a reputation.'

Then I was thrown out of the pit, landing at Sebastian's feet. I know Micka's name left my lips and I know what that did to Sebastian, but I couldn't help it. Lifting my head, I saw something that no child should ever see and that was my dad dead from that stupid Fae bitch. I hope she rots in hell.

Right now, I only want person and Sebastian has no other choice, but to grant my request and he's on his way. I've already heard the car, so I know that Clegg has let him in. Sebastian will be sulking, but I don't give a fuck. I need my real rock.

There's a knock on my door.

'Can I come in?'

Throwing open the door, I fall into his arms and he half carries me towards the bed where we both lay there together.

'Mina,' Jono whispers into my hair as I sob into his chest. 'Mina, let it out. Just let it go.'

I know he's also crying with me. We are both hurting together. My father became his when Danny went to prison. We shift position so that we are now laid together spooned.

'Why wouldn't they save him?' I ask.

'Because he was already gone. They can't bring him back from the dead. It's not their right,' Jono answers.

'But we are Marleys,' I whimper.

Jono pulls me closer to him and holds tighter. He smells so good. He must have just showered, because it's really strong. It's funny, it's something I've ever noticed before. The smell of masculinity.

'It's just a name, Mina. It's just a name.'

'I read the book,' I whisper.

'I know you did.'

'No, I mean, I read the book beneath the book.'

'I knew what you meant Mina, but you don't need to worry about that right now. Right now you've got to get through this.'

I turn so I'm facing him and see how puffed up and red his eyes are.

I'm not sure I can do this anymore?'

'You can,' he says.

'They all want too much.'

'Then give them only what you want them to have.'

I look at his face and see how much he has matured. I realise that I'm not the only one who has suffered this past year, he has too. Very much so and yet, we both have a long way to go. Reaching out, I stroke his face and hold my palm against his cheek. His eyes close briefly at my touch. The pulse of electricity flows from skin to skin causing both our breaths to catch. It's always been there, the chemistry between us. Both Marley bloodlines burning brightly when together. We are slowly folding into one another subconsciously, feeling a need.

'If they'd have asked us what they had of our parents, would you have?'

'What do you mean?'

'You know what I mean.'

The moment holds us, both staring into the other's eyes. The chemistry that we've always felt weaves around us and tightens its hold and both our bodies' starts to shake against the other. It's Jono who breaks it first.

'Turn over Mina,' he snaps, pushing me so that my back is now against him. 'I know you need comfort right now, but never ever try that with me again. I would walk away from you right now in order for us never to go there. We are not them. We are better.'

'Sorry,' I mutter.

Now I feel stupid. How could I have even thought it or allowed my Marley nature to take over. Jono is right, we are better than that.

'Just go to sleep Mina, for the love of god, just sleep.'

And I do. Fall into some endless dream world that feels just as bleak as the real one. I want to wake up, but then the scene changes and I'm in the gardens of the Manor and looking up at the statue that I now know is me. I used to find it an ugly thing, marred with ivy and moss, barely recognisable in its features. Yet, I do so myself in there.

There's a presence behind me and closing my eyes, I try and maintain some calm.

'It would have been ten times easier if you'd just told me,' I say.

'Would you have believed it if I had,' Gabriel says.

'No because according to Marleux you're a liar,' I snap.

'Coming from him that's a little rich.'

I give him a look and he sighs.

'Fine, I lied about the Militant...'

'His name is Micka,' I shout.

Gabriel takes a step back and even bows his head slightly.

'I'm sorry—Micka. I lied, because I needed to. What do you want me to say? You read the story. You know how hard it was for me not to give you whatever you wanted.'

'Am I really her?' I ask.

Gabriel looks up at the statue and sighs.

'You are you. Yes, you are reincarnation and part of her still lives on, but you are the Mina Marley that is loved and cherished, by this town.'

'And what about you? Do you love me?' I ask.

'Do you really want me to answer?'

'Yes I do. Be honest.'

'I will always love you, Mina, but I can never love you like I did then and what would be the point when your heart belongs to Micka. Think of it this way, Mina. You and I are in similar positions, we both love someone we cannot have and both have to make the sacrifice in order to put things right.'

'Will you tell me something honestly, Does Sebastian really love me or has it only ever been about possession?'

'I'm not doing this this way. Wake up!'

My eyes snap open and Jono is still sleeping beside me. I notice Gabriel's shadow in front of me and slowly remove myself from beneath Jono's arm.

'Come, let me take you home,' he says taking my hand.

'I'm not ready,' I start to say, only to find we are back at Mina's. It feels strange being here when it's closed and dark. Considering that I used to come down here a lot and just sit on nights I couldn't sleep. But that was almost a lifetime ago. Now this place is becoming alien to me.

Gabriel fusses behind the bar area and then returns with a large bottle of Jack and two tumblers.

'This isn't going to be good is it?' I ask.

He pours the drinks and nudges me towards one of the booths. Outside it has started to rain a little. I love the smell of a spring shower and the sound of it on the glass pane always brings me comfort and I hope it does now.

'I'm going to tell you the story of this town from the very beginning and when I am done then you will have all the answers you need. Are you ready for it?'

I nod.

'Are you sure, because once it is said then it cannot be unsaid?' he pushes.

'I'm sure.'

'Then I will begin.'

When this world was barely young there was only one race of humans. They had grown and evolved, becoming a breed in their own right. We as angels watched and guided them as the Powers commanded, but something happened. Something no one really knows, but it was suddenly decided that a new race of humans would be created and the other should die out. They would squeeze the life out of them until there was no other choice. This of course upset many of the angels, but what could they do.

So a piece of land was found and walled off from the humans and we all worked at making this into a place of perfection. A new start. The garden of purity and hope.

Seven days we toiled, the angels all worked their fingers to the bone. No matter your station, you worked, my brothers and sister and I were amongst them. But there were rumblings. From my brother mainly. He and his workers wanted to know why so much effort was going into this walled place when there were humans outside the wall that could be helped. But the Powers refused to answer his questions and told him that he must obey their will.

As you may have guessed that brother was Lucifer and you are fully aware of what happened there. But that was just the start and the war was some time after.

Anyway, on the seventh day, the garden was complete and the Powers were happy. They told us it was now time to introduce the new race of humans. Ones that would be so perfect and loyal that no other race would be needed. The race of God borne from one man and woman purely made.

The man was brought into the garden first. He was the image of perfection. Beautiful in every way. Tall, dark and sculptured, but you know this. You've seen with your own eyes. He was not called Sebastian then. His first name; his god given name was Adam. We were told that Adam's bride would come to him by the rising of the next sun and they would be tied as man and wife and be the parents of the new race. It was my job to fetch her and keep her safe until that time.

I was honoured and I knew my siblings were jealous, but I didn't care, our father trusted me with his new prize. So I went to the very outskirts of the walled garden and that's where I found you...her waiting. You had white blond hair then and deepest brown eyes. Beautiful is not even a word I could ever use. Your innocence shone through and as soon as you saw me, you threw question upon question at me. You wanted to see everything. Know everything.

I was forbidden of course to tell you anything, so I told you stories of another world where us angels lived and how blessed your life would be in this new land. You asked about the wall and I lied telling you that the world outside the wall had not been finished and until that day, this was your home.

But I had no idea how much the curiosity burned inside you. It was as though the Powers hadn't thought that through. A tiny mistake on their part and on my part it was to fall asleep. After seven days of working on that damned garden, I was exhausted and fell asleep.

When I awoke, you had gone and I knew instantly that you'd climbed the wall. Frightened of the consequences, I climbed to the other side and searched for you. It didn't take me long and what I found caused me to wail in grief and panic. That filthy demon Marleux was defiling you beneath an apple tree. You barely whimpered, just laid there frozen. With a scream, I sent Marleux back to hell, but the damage was already done. I could see it in your eyes. The innocence gone.

Carrying you back over the wall, I found a stream and cleaned you the best I could. I had no idea if the Powers knew, and if they did, why didn't they stop that creature. But all I did know was that I was in trouble. Desperate trouble and as the night passed and you laid in my arms, I knew then that no matter what I would make sure I kept you safe.

At the rising of the sun, I woke you and told you that your husband waited, but you refused to go. You told me that you loved only me and that I was the only husband you wanted. That I could lay with you just as the demon had done.

'But I am angel and you are human. You are made for Adam and that is God's will.'

'But what about what I want?' you asked. 'You call him Adam, but do not give me my name. Am I his property? Am I owned by this Adam and never to be free?'

It had been expressly forbidden for me to give you your name. It was to be part of the bonding. Adam would give his wife her name and make her his. You were both made equals and would rule together as such, but Adam's right was to give you your name.

'You say I am his equal, yet he gives me my name. Why can I not choose my own?'

'And what name would you choose?' I asked hoping that by calling your bluff it would delay your argument.

It worked, a sulky pout formed on your face and it caused me to smile.

'How are you are feeling after last night?' I dared myself to ask.

You shrugged at me. 'I know I should never have gone over the wall and I paid the price for my disobedience, but why would you lie about a world that is just as beautiful outside?'

I looked at you shocked. 'You were raped by an ungodly creature and you still think that world is beautiful?'

This time you looked at me puzzled. 'What does that word mean? Rape?'

'It means you were forced against your will,' I answered.

'But he asked me to lie down and I did. He asked me if he could touch me and I said yes. I felt something deep inside when he came to me and I wanted him to have me, so I allowed it.'

Shocked, I pulled you to a stop and causing a wince as I gripped onto you tightly.

'You are made by the great Powers that Be. My father is your father and he made you pure and with love. You must never speak of this to anyone. You will go to your husband and lie with him as a virgin. Your encounter with the demon must never be revealed and if it is already known, then it was rape.'

'But I don't…'

I pulled you closer and played the only card I had to hand.

'If you love me as you claim then you will do as I ask and I swear that you will always be under my protection. But if you reveal, then I will be killed as well as you.'

So, I took you to Adam where the angels and the Powers waited. They all loved you instantly. Why wouldn't they? And Adam could barely take his eyes off you. The binding was done and he gave you your name and it was Eve.

Months passed and I was called back to do my own work to start with my brothers, the demise of the other race. We thought we'd left you both happy and content. Ready to start a new breed of perfect humans.

How wrong I was?

As soon as you called my name, I knew something was wrong. Your swelling stomach gave me false hope and did not make sense with the tears in your eyes.

'Why do you cry, child?' I asked.

'I cannot lay with my husband. He commands me to lie still on my back, but I find it uncomfortable. I want to join in with him as I did before, but he will not allow it and he's failing.'

'What do you mean failing?'

With damp brown eyes you looked up at me.

'I try and do what he asks. I try and lay still, but nature takes over and it causes him to fail. Now my belly grows, but we both know that he cannot have made that happen. He demands that I die and he's asking the Powers to allow it.'

Vomit stung my throat. That damned demon had put his seed into my father's prize and you were going to pay the price for it. Deciding that I would have to face this for us both, I told you to hide and wait for my return and made my way to where Adam and the Powers waited.

'Where is the girl, Gabriel?' they asked.

'She waits for the verdict, but does not understand her crime,' I said.

'That whore carries another's child in her womb,' Adam spat.

'And who's would that be Adam?' I asked. 'There is only you here and only you that have lain with her. So tell me, where the child has come from?'

Adam looked at me flabbergasted and stumped. He had no idea of the world beyond the wall and his argument was flawed by the lack of knowledge, but the Powers knew and with a wave of a hand they sent Adam into a slumber.

'We know that the child is not Adam's,' they said. 'She must be destroyed and another will be made. Adam will never know.'

'But why destroy her? Why not allow him to believe that child is his?' I asked.

'Because she stinks of hell, that child's father is demon and must be destroyed. She has defiled the gift given to her and you have allowed that to happen.'

I have no idea what made me say what I did, but all I knew was that I had to protect you and give us both time to escape.

'The child is not demon. The child is mine. I raped her and covered my scent with that of a demon to save myself. I never expected a child.'

'You lie,' the Powers said.

I raised my head to sky and yelled to my father: 'The child she carries is mine. I raped her and made her my own because I love her. Please spare her and take my life instead.'

As soon as the words were spoken the Powers disappeared. My father calling them to discuss what would be done. They couldn't just strike me down. I was the one of the first sons of heaven. Things had to be done right. But I didn't have a lot of time, so I ran to where you were and told you what I'd said.

'You can't stay here. You have to leave and go over the wall,' I told you. 'This place is no longer your home. You have your freedom.'

'What about you?' she asked.

'I will be fine, I swear.'

'And my baby?'

'When it is your time I will be there. This baby will be the start of something new for you. Go and be free and be happy, but never cross this wall again.'

You threw your arms around me and kissed my cheek. Then with a lift from me, you straddled the wall.

'I know what my name will be,' you shouted.

'And pray what will it be?' I smiled.

'Lilith.'

And you disappeared over that wall and months later I was there to watch the first red haired girl and dark haired boy to be born. The first of the Marley line, born and hidden in my protection.

I look at Gabriel dumbfounded and grabbing the bottle, I drink from it neat. I knew some of this already, but to hear his side is flooring me. He put himself in the firing line in order to allow a past me escape death.

'What happened next? To you. To Sebastian or Adam?' I ask.

'My father of course knew what I'd done, but forgave me because I was prepared to sacrifice myself for one of his own. Plus another of his sons was causing bigger problems. Adam, however, was harder to convince. While he slept, the gardens were changed again and made fresh.

He got his new Eve, made from parts of his body in order to make the bond stick, but he knew deep down that something was wrong, but didn't know what. When Eve bore Cain, he still believed that child was not his and took him to the gardens to kill him. It was then, he was told everything. Flying into an even bigger fury, he swore he would kill his whole family. That was when the deal was struck.

We told him that he would be given immortality and when the Lilith was born again in another thousand years, he would have her again. Pure and ready to be his wife.'

'And once he had his wife, then what? We live happily ever after?'

Gabriel nods. 'Something like that. Now you know. We gave him a brand new wife and a new start and he fathered a whole nation of humans, but he was willing to stop that because he loved you.'

'What I don't understand is why the Others are all interested in me? What do they care what Sebastian and I do?'

'When you left the garden, work was already being done to kill off the other race of humans. My brothers massacred them, but you took the role of champion. You, had other ideas. You told those you could of the garden and what the angels were doing.

Those who believed you scattered and hid from us. Due to your children, some of Marleux's power rubbed off onto you. That little magic, you give power with those that scattered and that was the start of what we now know as the Others. The ones from beyond the wall. You saved the first Otherworldlies from us angels and your protection meant that we couldn't touch them as long as they stayed out of the walled garden.'

'And where is this walled garden now?' I ask.

Gabriel sighs and pours himself another glass.

'The walled garden is everywhere apart from this place. There are other small towns that you secured from us, but Supton is the world of the Others. The Powers squeezed as much as they could and finally gave in and allowed this place to be left. The Manor is where Marleux took you. This place here is where you and I stayed together that first night. That is why you are so drawn to both places. It's the place of your birth so to speak. That is why we ask you to go back. It's a power source and it's the reason Williamina didn't want you to have it.'

'And that's why they must become human to leave this place?'

Gabriel nods. Silence falls between us. He's told me a lot and a lot about the relationship between us both. Our connection that I do feel, but seems dulled this time round.

'I'm still in love with Micka,' I say finally.

'I know,' he answers.

'Why do I love Micka and not you? Why are you not part of this fucked up love triangle?'

Gabriel sighs. 'Because you are only a reincarnation of Lilith. You have been brought up to know your own heart and mind. You love with your own heart, Mina not with Lilith's. But you must be with Sebastian. The Powers command it. He must have his wife. He cannot be immortal much longer.'

'I will do as you ask. I will marry Sebastian and be his wife, but never ask me to remain faithful. I will choose that path for myself.'

Gabriel nods in agreement. He knows there's no other choice for him or them. I have to keep some of my own terms. I may always be faithful to Sebastian, but I don't want them to know that.

The sun is rising in the distance and Gabriel tells me that it's time to take me back.

'What happened to Eve?' I ask suddenly.

'Eve died naturally with all her children around her. She knew he didn't love her, but she was made to honour and obey and that's what she did to the very last breath.'

'What happened with the whole apple fiasco?' I ask.

Gabriel gave me a small smirk.

'Pure fable. The apple tree is your story not Eve's.'

Dragging myself out of the booth, I stretch and finish off the Jack in my glass. It's hard for me to explain, but I feel much better about Gabriel than I ever did. He has put up with so much in order to make sure I lived.

Gabriel touches my arm and we are back in my room where Jono still slumbers. So much for missing me.

'Thank you for being honest,' I say.

'You are welcome, oh and Mina, leave your cousin alone,' he smirks.

Going Home

Mina Online Blog 7ᵗʰ June 2330

The silence at the breakfast table is deafening. Sebastian, Jono and I are all eating awkwardly. I've already apologised to Jono about my behaviour and he just hugged me and made me swear never to do it again. Of course I'll never try it again. It was probably the last remnants of what I went through. Although, I still don't understand what happened. Personally, I think it was a build-up of all that power and I broke down. If I'd been human I'd have probably curled up in a corner and cried, but having the power of heaven and hell inside me caused an eruption.

I don't really remember much about what happened after Micka turned up and freaking out, reading that book. It's just a blur of mixed up images. Where flashes of colours and bad feelings come back and my brain just pushes them back down.

I feel very different this morning. Numb and it doesn't help that by the looks on the men's faces they are expecting something more from me. More tears or hysterics, but I can't bring myself to do anything. Numb is all I feel and with that feeling, I've no idea what to do. I mean I know that I have a funeral to arrange and loads of paper work. No doubt everything just falls into my hands. But I don't care a damn about doing any of it. In fact, I just want to be left alone.

'I want to go home?'

Both Sebastian and Jono look up at me.

'This is your home, Mina,' Sebastian says.

'No, my flat is my home and I want to go back.'

'It's not wise for you to be alone right now,' he pushes.

'Sebastian is right, just stay here for a little longer and then see how you feel,' Jono adds.

'I already know how I feel,' I insist.

Getting to my feet, I leave the table and make my way upstairs where Sebastian catches up with me.

'Why are you pushing me away?' he asks.

'My father has just died,' I say.

'I'm aware. I was there,' he says.

Tension is growing between us and the chasm feels like its expanding. Even though I know that Gabriel lied about Micka and I's future, I can't go back on my word with Sebastian. I was made for him. My perfect fit. The soul mate everyone wants. I have to marry him and the love I do have will sustain us until the end. But right now I need some space from him. From everyone. Just to get my head together.

'Will it make you feel better if I tell you that I still want to marry you?'

Sebastian looks at me for a moment but his defensive stance has fallen slightly.

'The fact that you've just said that to me makes me think otherwise. Maybe it's time we just gave up on this idea of us being together. I'm tired of fighting for you.'

He turns away from me and I'm shocked he's giving up now. After all this time he's willing to just let me go. But I'm tired too. Exhausted.

'Why wasn't Eve good enough for you?' I ask.

He stops and turns my way. His face pale and angry.

'Gabriel,' he hisses. 'He told you.'

'I read the book,' I answer.

'The book only told you that you were the Primum. The first woman of the new human race. The woman of god. It never told you about Eve,' he snaps.

'He thought I had the right to know and I do. You had plenty of time to tell me who I was to you and about Eve.'

'Plenty of time,' he laughs 'Mina, I've barely had time to tell you anything. I've barely had time to even enjoy you as my partner. There's always been something in the way.'

'Are you blaming me?' I throw back.

'Well you were the one who fell in love with everyone else. Even now, you share a bed with your Marley cousin rather than with me.'

'I do love you. I don't know how many times I have to say this to you. I wanted Jono in my bed because I needed my family.'

'So you didn't try it on with him?'

Shock registers on my face. I know for a fact, Jono would never say anything.

'I know everything that goes on under my roof, which is why I know you disappeared with Gabriel.'

'So you're spying on me now?' I shout.

'You *will* marry me, Mina I know that much is true, but to say that you will never remain faithful cuts like a knife.'

'You have to understand, I have to do this on my terms. You've all taken all my power away. I need to take some of it back. That is all I meant,' I argue.

'I'm trying to understand what you're going through,' he pushes.

'You will never know what I feel, because you will never have a father,' I spit, before I whisper an apology.

His face tells me he doesn't believe me and there's nothing more I can do. Pushing past him, I make my way upstairs to get my stuff, and with Jono, I leave the Manor and return home.

'You don't have to do this. You can always stay with me,' Jono offers.

'No, I need to do this. It's my home and I have to grow up and face things.'

Jono sighs. 'Okay, but you call if you need me. The funeral home is going to want to speak to you soon, make sure you call me at least with that.'

I promise and then climb out of the car. Mina's is closed because people are still in shock and don't want to see me never mind eat at my place. Going to the back door, I unlock it and step inside. It feels cold and lifeless, but I have to do this. The door to the hidden stairwell waits for me and taking a deep breath I reach out and open it.

I can do this. The flat is my home. The safest place I've known for years. The climb up that staircase feels heavy and hard work, but I'm soon at the front door and with a deep breath the door is open and I'm in my flat for the first time in months.

It's incredibly tidy. Pristine even. I don't even remember leaving it this way. Micka and I left in such a hurry; there was no time to bother.

'I thought it best to tidy.'

I jump at Uz's voice and without a second thought run straight into his arms and hold him tight. I wanted to be angry with him. I was ready for it, but I can't. Not after what he did for me. His body tenses at first before arms are wrapped around me.

'I thought you would hate me,' I say choking on sobs.

'Why would I hate you, Mina?' he asks.

119

'Because what I made you do. What you saw. What you did…'

'Shush Mina, please don't go there. I only did what was needed. You tested me beyond even my limits. Because I love you and because of Ray…'

Now his voice cracks. His best friend. The man and angel who was at his side for however long is gone.

'I was angry that you didn't bring him back,' I say.

'I know. But understand that I couldn't, no angel can. We can heal, but only one thing can bring the dead back legitimately.'

'I should not have expected you to. You've done enough already.'

'What happens now?' I ask.

Sitting down, he proceeds to tell me what happens next when it comes to my father. All Others must return to their home land when they die. But my father was a condemned angel. It's not easy for those angels. Their divinity is gone once they fall, yet their bodies are special and shouldn't be left in the human soil.

When it comes to my father, it has been decided that his body will be buried in Supton within the grounds of our home. This is the Powers gift to me. First, however, the paper trail of my father's identity in the human world will be washed away and only those within this town will know he existed. This is the way of things and knowing it makes me breathe a lot easier.

Jaq's Email to Carla 7th June 1030 hrs

Hey Hun,

I know mum would have already told you about Ray. I just can't get my head around it. Any of it. I was with the rest of the town outside Ray's when it happened. In fact, Jono had managed to pull me away from the crowd and we'd argued about my relationship with Dom. He said that he loved me and we should be together.

'You deserve more than what that Necro can give you.'

Of course I kick off. I hate that he calls Dom that. He's more than what he was born. But the other complication isn't helping. If I am pregnant with Jono's baby then I can't do that to Dom. But I'm not sure that I can walk away from him. Not when I love him so much. It's so messed up.

But there we were arguing, when there was an almighty roar and the ground trembled beneath us.

'She's opening the portal to hell,' Jono whispered.

Then there was the most horrendous silence and stillness. We all had to wait and see, and knowing Mina was in the midst of that and hanging over hell scared me shitless. Then it all kicked off when we heard that someone was dead. My heart stopped as both Jono and I mouthed Mina's name. But when they pulled Ray's body from the house, Jono nearly buckled as he pushed his way through the crowd.

I didn't see Mina, I expect that they zapped her out of there to the Manor and I've not seen her since.

Now we are waiting for the funeral arrangements and to see what will happen to my second dad. I'm not sure if I should call Mina. What do I say to her? Does she even want to speak to me after what happened between us? Can I just say sorry and it be over? Things have really become messed up between us and if I take the test that is hiding in my bottom drawer then it could get ten times worse. Carla, I really could do with your help right now.

Much Love

Jaq

Candice's Journal May 7th 2330hrs

Uncle Edwin came to see me again. It seems he and Freda are worried about me and feel that a few things need to be settled between us as a family. It was felt that the treatment of me and my father was unjust and that they should have and could have done more.

I've given up being angry with the rest of the Roses, purely because I now have some idea of my own self-worth. I wonder if they know that the Royal Family are interested and that's why they are now stepping forward. But no matter what fucking front I put on, I still want to be accepted as part of their family.

'I did love your father, I just never really understood him,' Edwin says. 'He was a troubled young man with an awful amount of power that he couldn't control.'

'The power that I have and Nanna?' I ask.

'Nowhere near that. But he had a gift. When he met your mother he seemed to calm down, but they were both so young and when you came, that pressure was too much. That's when we should have stepped up, but didn't. We had our own brood to care for.'

'Are you asking for my forgiveness?'

'We are Roses. We only give forgiveness if we see fit to give it.'

I can't help but smile at that truth. You can ask us all you want, but at the end of the day we only give what's deserved.

'I want us to move on,' I say finally.

'Then that's what we will do starting with a family meal.'

We promise to meet after the funeral of course, because he tells that my cousin, Jaq is struggling. I know she will be less inclined to welcome me into the fold. I've been closer to Mina than she and she must know by now that her best friend and I are connected on some form or spiritual level. I'm no longer the waste of space cousin. I'm someone. I can hold my head up high and say I'm Candice Rose.

East of Eden

Tannini's Journal 10th June 2330hrs

Ray's paperwork is more or less sorted and we are close to making him disappear from the human world. His funeral arrangements have already been put in place. It seems Mina is on a mission to get things sorted. I know the reason why. If she's busy then she's not thinking about what's happened. It's the reason she's opened Mina's.

'Keep me busy' mentality. The problem with that is it don't work. It bites you in the arse eventually.

I, however, have other things to focus on. The fact that the Roberts girl and her demon forefather have disappeared. They are our links to the Emandato, who are still as elusive as ever. Tyia was very close to that leader, but with her in Hell, I won't be getting information out of her that's for sure. The angel at the top of that chain needs to be found and I've even resorted to calling Gabriel. But it seems he's either as clueless as we are or doesn't want to get involved.

'No-one will go near Mina if I can help it,' he says.

'Well you've done a smart job so far. They've nearly had her three times already,' I answer.

Of course this didn't go down too well, with the archangel.

My second problem is the Council and the pressure they are putting on Beverley. They know about the two of us and majorly pissed off with her. She's on the verge of being fired by them or worse. I've not seen or heard from her for days and I'm beyond myself with worry. Fuck me, I'm inlove with the girl and the thought of her in danger messes with my head.

How in earth did I get into this mess? I yearn for the days when I was a single man and didn't give a fuck about anyone. Then I come back to this town and my life changes. This place is going to finish me, I'm sure.

Mina's online blog 10th June 2200hrs

It's a slow day at the diner, because still no one wants to really come in. I've had the usual condolences, but no one wants to really to be near me either. However, in the afternoon my day slowly starts to get worse when Candice arrives on my doorstep.

I swear that she is changing right before my eyes. Her black costumes are not as flamboyant, but almost like Christine, in her floaty hippy clothes. Then there's her whole presence and demeanour. There's less arrogance, but more humble, but in wise and knowing way. It instantly pisses me off, because I know full well that she will know my tale and has been part of keeping it from me.

So she comes in, but instead of looking at me like she usually does, I note that she's uncomfortable. This is new. What does she know now?

'What do you want?' I sigh.

There's a frown and puzzlement on her face, which in turns must reflect in my own.

'Can we talk…in the back?' she says.

Nodding, I tell Vicki that I'll be just in my office and then lead the way. Once closed up in my office, I wait for Candice to say whatever's on her mind again.

'Is this anything to do with Lorreli or me being the Primum?' I ask.

'No, this is nothing to do with that. I came to apologise and offer my condolences.'

She's still not looking at me.

'What have you got to be sorry for?'

'Don't you remember?'

I shake my head. I don't remember much.

'Your dad, Ray, he jumped in front of me to stop that Fae bitch's magic. He died saving me.'

I can tell by the way her body tenses that she expects some sort of violent reaction. But I can't. I know my father and he was an angel. It's what they do. Put themselves in the firing line in order to save.

'I don't blame you. There was so much shit going on. We all did what we could.'

'Micka was inside me,' Candice blurts out.

My body tenses at his name and the reference. Of course I knew. The way he shouted through Candice was enough for me to know.

'He still loves you so much,' she continues.

'Candice, please…'

'As soon as his essence was inside me, I felt every hurt and pain he's suffering.'

'Enough.'

'Mina, you can't deny what went on between you,' she pushes.

'Enough!'

The ground shakes beneath our feet and there's a sudden downpour of hail stones. The power I have is getting stronger. It ripples through my body like electricity and it's addictive.

'No! *You* will fucking listen,' she slams and there's a large crack of lightening that makes my windows rattle.

I take a step back as she raises an eyebrow at me. This is new and interesting.

'I can do that sort of tantrum too,' she smirks.

'Fine, I'll sit.'

We both sit and take a moment to get our breath back. This is the first time where I've consider the level playing field Candice and I are actually on. She is my equal.

Sitting there she tells me that I've unfinished business with Micka. Of course she's right. We were living together, sleeping together as one, and then I walked out on him. Made him fall in love before ripping him in two and yet, he still comes back. Still saves me.

'I've said my piece;' she says finally, 'the rest is up to you.'

She leaves me alone and getting to my feet, I leave my office and up to the flat. I don't know if I'm able to call him like I do Uz. I don't think I've ever done it. Standing my front room, I open my mouth, but nothing comes out, because I know he's already there—sitting on his bed—waiting.

Opening the bedroom door, my heart leaps and drops. He still has that affect and it frustrates me. I can't remember what life was like before him and its exhausting trying to get back to that. Be that Mina and not this woman I've turned into it.

'We need to talk,' he says.

That at least is obvious, but where do we start? What do say to each other? Because nothing can change. We can't be together.

'I'm not sure what can be said.'

I sit down beside him and his heat stretches towards me. It causes me to lean close and I have to force myself into a static position.

'I tried to stay away from you, but the need to protect you was far too strong,' he says.

'I'm grateful, I swear. I never meant to hurt you.'
'I know.'

'I can't cope with being what they all want me to be.'

'And what is that, Mina?' he asks.

'The Primum,' I answer.

Micka sighs and turns to face me. Those blue eyes looking deep into my soul, like they have a thousand times before. But nothing prepares me for what he says next.

'I was sent to kill you.'

'What?'

'When you were Lilith. When Gabriel allowed you to escape, the Powers sent me to destroy you.'

'And why didn't you?' I choke out.

I can barely breathe now. This angel that has spent most of this year protecting and risking life and limb for me was originally my assassin.

'Gabriel hid you far too well. I could never find you. You were hidden from all angels apart from him.'

'So what changed? Why were you chosen to be my godfather?'

'You must understand, Mina, how I'm made. I am a Militant, which means I do as I'm told, even more than all other angels. Gabriel and Sebastian knew that by giving me to you, it eliminated anyone using me to kill you again.'

'They are good at using loopholes,' I muse. 'So what changed? What has changed in your make-up that makes you disobey? What if you want to kill me again?' my voice rises in panic and I feel an arm come around me.

'You know the answer to those questions. You changed me. I will never hurt you Mina, because I love you. I am not the same angel I was then.'

'But you could still…'

'I will never hurt you.'

Snuggling further into his arms, I know it's the truth. It's the reason I feel so safe with him. He squeezes me tighter and with it are all the memories of why I love him the first place. Lifting my face, I turn it towards his and our eyes meet. Then something strange happens. He looks at me and a frown deepens.

'Things have changed,' he says and then disappears.

Well at least that hasn't changed. He still leaves me wanting more and wondering what he's thinking.

Candice's Journal 10th June 2245hrs

'Did you help me do that?' I ask Lorreli.

'No, you did that,' she replies. 'I no longer hold any control over you.'

That shocks me, I didn't realise that Lorreli's hold had gone. I could have expelled her long ago, but haven't. It's like I feel her smile at my thoughts of expelling her. She knows I wouldn't. We are one now and the thought of being without her is scary as fuck.

'So, that's what I can do now? Control the elements?'

'You and Mina are connected you know that. You feel it when you're together. Feeding each other, but it can also cause you to react against the other.'

I knew when I found Nanna's book that Mina was special and powerful, I'd thought she was Canaan, but now I know she's Lilith the first woman of God's race. The Primum.

Little is really known about her, not even in the human world. It's like she became the worst thing after Lucifer. The female demon of all demons. The fact is that she was never a demon, she just got knocked up by one. She was made in perfection. The image that the Powers wanted. Call me bitchy, but looking at Mina, it's hard to imagine that she is THAT Lilith. I mean she's hardly perfection. A little chunky and short. Not exactly model or movie star. Shit! I could be more Lilith than she.

'Candice,' Lorreli warns. 'You're better than that.'

I mutter an apology.

'So who am I?'

'You will know very soon.'

And that's all I get, before she switches off and I hear no more. Okay, so we are playing that game. I will find out even if I've to go back to Faeterra. I'm sure they will know who I really am to Mina, because not matter how many times I look at the story of Lilith and the creation of God's race, I don't see how I fit in. Maybe the answer is staring me right in the face, and I'm too close to see it.

Mina's Online Blog 12th June 2130hrs.

'So now you know,' Danny says to me.

I decided it was time that I went to see my uncle. I'd dragged Jono with me. A family get-together that is desperately needed, because they're all I've got at the end of the day and we need each other. So in Danny's small bedsit, the three remaining Marleys sit and talk.

'I take it I was the last to know,' I answer.

'Hey, I didn't know,' Jono puts in. 'I thought we were just sex demons.'

'We had to be sure first,' Danny says. 'We made a big mistake with your mother.'

'How can you make a mistake? Didn't you all just know?' I ask.

'If it were that simple then your mother wouldn't have got hurt like she did.'

His tone tells me not to push it. My mother is a sore subject to my uncle and he hates talking about her. I suppose to watch your twin sister suffer and die is harder than anything he's gone through.

'Well, now I know I'm this Lilith, I'm not sure what I'm supposed to do? With all the Elders all coming here, they are obviously expecting something from me.'

'Just be you, Mina. You are only an incarnate. You don't have to make the same choices as Lilith. You are also not your mother,' Danny says.

'If I were you, I'd stick by Sebastian. It seems he has the power to keep you safe,' Jono adds.

'You do know that Sebastian is nothing but a human man,' Danny snaps.

'He's immortal,' Jono argues.

'Not now. Your cousin here has ended that gift.'

'Guys, please don't argue. I need you both to be with me. I know you don't like Sebastian, Danny, but I am still going to marry him. Jono is right, until we know who leads the Emandato then I need to keep safe. But for now, I really need to get the next few days over with.'

Both men hang their heads. In the midst of all the Emandato stuff and me being Lilith, Ray's funeral is taking a back seat.

'Have you any idea what the angels have decided?'

I knew they'd want to know, and all I can tell them is what Uz has told me.

'The Powers have chosen not to take his essence back. We bury his body, but as for his soul, it will be dispensed off as though he didn't exist.'

'What a bunch of jumped up pricks,' Danny hisses.

'Well according to Uz, it's because he fell,' I shrug. 'But to be honest, I don't really care. I'd rather no one got it. His memory is all I need.'

This brings silence before they grab into some form of Marley group hug. It starts of forced, before we fall into a natural hug.

Jono then tells us that he needs to return to the city and that the promoters want him back and working. So I know that straight after Ray's funeral, my cousin will be gone again. I could argue with him to stay, but he has his own life to lead outside of this town. As we get ready to leave, Danny pulls me to one side.

'Mina, I need you to promise me one thing.'

'What?'

'Promise me that when you become Mrs Daniels that you will continue to control your own life. Your mother wouldn't want it any other way.'

I smile. 'Don't worry I will always be a Marley.'

Time to Say Goodbye

Tannini's Journal 14th July 2130hrs

Well, it's finally arrived. The day that the whole town has been dreaded. Then there's lil' Mina. I've no idea what's going on with her, because she's avoiding me. I know why. I'm the closest thing to Ray and it's a reminder she doesn't want.

But this day has turned into more than the funeral of my best friend, it's been the day when the past as returned to me and Supton twice over.

In the early morning, I'd taken a long run around the town to clear my head. After Williamina's attack at the start of the cycle, the town went into hiding and were afraid, but this morning, the atmosphere is different. Heavy and sad. But one of their own is gone and about to be put in the ground. All thoughts will be of course on Mina, but each town's folk will be remembering Ray in their own way.

I've heard on the grapevine that the angels won't be taking Ray's soul. That's one hell of a slap in the face. That man was at their beck and call, even give them his only child to fuck over and they won't take his soul. It will go to Aides like everyone else.

I know that angels do get sent to Aides, but after everything he did surely the rules could be bent. It's not like they have broken the rules before   Well, I bet Ray wouldn't want them to have it anyhow.

Beverley finally got in touch with me, but it was hurried and garbled. She told me that she was fine and that I was not to contact her. It was over. She couldn't risk her career to be with me. I don't believe her. There were hidden messages in the call.

One that was telling me to wait. Be patient. So that's what I'm doing. I'm allowing her the space to do what she needs to and then she'll come to me.

After my run and shower, I had no choice to put on my black suit and make my way towards the Manor.

Mina's Online Blog 14ᵗʰ July 2230hrs.

It was one of those mornings, where I didn't want to wake up and again I was in Micka's bed. Not with him, but still in his bed. Sebastian's ring is on my finger and yet I still keep my ex lover's bed warm. You see, as Lilith, I'm still no wiser who has my heart.

But today is more important than my love life. It's a day where I'd hoped to be older when I did this, but some bitch with a vendetta robbed me of that choice. Climbing out of bed, I see the hanging black dress I've chosen to wear. Sebastian is meeting me later. I spoke to him last night, made the effort to allow him to help me. Learn to be more giving towards him, whether I want to or not. He will be my husband after all.

The shower does little to relieve the tension. I feel like I should be doing something other than waiting. Downstairs is off limits. An order from the Roses. They, with Craig and Dom are preparing the food for the Wake.

'Just rest and get yourself ready and leave us to worry,' Mrs Rose said.

I try and watch some TV to take my mind off the ticking clock, but it's not working and instead decide to dress and do my hair to distract myself. It's the best I can do. In fact the best I can do is probably hide myself in here and not go. They don't need me. I don't want to see them put him in the ground, because that means he really has gone and left me to fend for myself. The heiress to the Marley legacy and whatever that is.

The relationship I had with my father was always loving, but with an edge to it. Almost like opposing forces trying to grate and force ourselves together. I didn't know then the secret he was holding on to and just thought he was being an overbearing parent. I now know the freedom he did give. What the Powers wanted from me as woman. A pure woman and yet he allowed me to make that choice by myself. Yes I gave it to that waste of manhood Jimmy, but it was my choice. There were times I really resented him and what he asked from me, but with those same choices, I'd probably lie in order to protect a child of my own. Now, I've no idea who I'll go to. Danny? Uz? Will the angels even bother with me now I'm with Sebastian?

The funeral is being taken care of by the town undertakers, the Grundles. They've been nothing but kind and supportive. Again one of the Grundles girls was in my year at school—although she rarely mixed with anyone. The family are human and it's hard for humans living within Supton. Often they feel like outsiders. Jono—up until recently believed that he was human and would often comment that he felt like the dud Marley, because I had an angel father.

There's no need for the human residents to feel that way, in my mind. We are all in this world together. However, Margot Grundle was always stranger than most, and it's her and her father that came to speak to me. It was then that I realised that as adults we are still very different. I suppose working with the dead all the time leaves no room for glam and colour. Black and grey still drips off her. Not that I can talk about looks or dress sense.

All too soon, Margot is at my door telling me that they are ready for me. Grabbing my black jacket, I leave the security of my flat. My hand shakes as I fumble with the lock and realise I'm scared. Scared of saying goodbye. A hand touches mine and

Margot gives me a smile as she takes the key from me.

'I'll lock it,' she says. 'And take a moment to breathe.'

The small act of kindness pulls at my conscious after the things I've thought about her. Getting to the bottom of the stairs into the back of Mina's, I expect to go through the front, but instead she steers me to the back. I know this is so I don't see the work the Roses have done inside. But nothing prepares me for what happens when we round the corner.

In front of Mina's, the whole town stands in a sea of black and the sight catches my throat. But then what makes me stagger slightly is the black horse drawn corsage with my father in, laden with lilies.

'I didn't order this,' I whisper.

'No, Mr Daniels did,' Margot whispers.

I look at her and try and nod, but once again I feel annoyed. Why can't he just leave me to it?

'They are waiting. Do you remember what we said?' she asks.

'Yes, but I want Danny and Jono beside me, not Sebastian.'

I expect an argument, but a small smile warms her face.

'As you wish.'

She leaves me to go towards her father and instructs him of my request. He looks nervous, but just nods and waves me over. I stand behind the corsage with my eyes fixed on the pine box and I hear some frustrated murmurs from behind me. There's nothing Sebastian can do. He won't make a show in front of the town, so he'll give me my way.

'You chose your time to piss him off,' Danny says coming to my side.

'It will teach him to interfere,' I snap.

Jono's hand goes into mine and I take Danny's.

'Let's do this.'

With a nod to Margot, the corsage starts its slow ascent through the town up towards my family home. Every step is heavy and I can barely hear anyone elses. If it's not for the feel of Danny and Jono's hand in mine, then I'd be convinced I'm alone.

Concentrating on the box in front of me, it's hard to imagine that something so small holds someone like my father. A sudden thought of the box being empty invades my thoughts and I shake it away. The lack of noise is giving me too much time to think and that's not good. That's the last thing I need is to think. The sound of the horses hooves are hypnotic and find I'm counting each step. Keeping my mind occupied.

The path to the house is on an incline and the ache in my already heavy legs is growing in intensity. I can see the house in the distance and paralysis suddenly strikes me, bringing the whole precession to a stop, luckily a short sharp shout from Margot stops the horse.

'Mina, sweetheart, you need to carry on,' Danny says.

'I don't want to.'

'You have to. People need you to keep moving.'

'Danny, I don't care,' I hiss.

'Mina look at me,' Jono says forcing my eyes to his.

'Jonathan, don't,' Danny warns.

But Jono raises his hand to silence him. I start to feel the Marley pull run through my body in warm waves and my palpating heart slows down a notch.

Deborah.C.Foulkes

It's not as heated as when we were laid together, but the attraction is still there.

'Mina, we are going to climb this hill to the top and then we will be there. Just a little further. Will you do what I ask?'

I shake my head stubbornly and try and fight his charm with my own. But I've not really the strength.

'Don't push it too far,' Danny hisses.

Jono wraps his arms around my waist which causes my body stretch against his and there are murmurs from behind. It must be some time since they've seen the Marleys in action.

I can just about hear in the distance somewhere, Sebastian asking what's going on and Danny telling him to back off. But the green in Jono's eyes are the only thing I'm focused on.

'Mina, you will do what I tell you to because you love me as I love you. Now walk up that hill.'

'Yes,' I whisper and slowly he lets me go and with a nudge and a slight drag by the hand, we are on the move again. The road takes us through the woods and even they are silent. Nothing, but dead air.

We pass the gates and the last leg of the precession will take us to the land behind the house, which I would always call a meadow. There's a place beneath a willow tree chosen. I know he loved that tree. There waiting for us is Uz with another angel in a dark suit who I don't know, but I'm told that he is the one they send for these sorts of things. I didn't even bother asking his name, because I didn't care. Beside them is Micka and my heart flinches painfully. Another unexpected surprise.

The corsage stops finally and Margot tells me to move to one side and that's when another surprise hits me and it threatens to tip me over the edge. I fully expected the pall bearers to lift my father, but none of them move, instead, Danny, Jono, Uz, Tannini, Micka and Sebastian step forward. Margot hurries some instruction to them and I find I'm rocking on the balls of my feet. Desperate to keep steady as they prepare to lift my father to his final resting place.

A hand touches mine and looking up I smile with relief at having a familiar face. Jaq looks at me with watery eyes and gives me a slow nod.

'I've got you,' she whispers.

'Thank you,' I mouth.

The men all lift my father with ease and slowly we all make the last walk to the graveside beneath the willow.

The coffin is placed on a raised plinth beside the dug grave and we all take our places. The angel that Uz informs me is called Simiel, stands at the head of the grave with Uz and Micka on either side. He starts to speak words, but I'm not hearing anything. It's something Archaic and old, which I assume is some form of blessing. Then he nods towards Tannini, who steps forward to talk about my father as a man.

I've not really been to see Tannini since, because I have no idea what to say to him. To be honest just hearing the obligatory sorry is too much. How are you supposed to respond to that? All that end up coming out is *it's okay* when really it isn't, but what can you say? The truth?

But I know Tannini too well and he's very giving when it comes to the truth and I don't need that right now. It will sting no doubt that I've not been in touch, but I'm sure he understands.

As he starts to talk, the summer blossom from neighbouring trees fill the air in the breeze and I soak in their scent trying with all my might to calm my turning insides. It's warming quickly and I find I'm shifting uncomfortably in my dress. Lifting my eyes, I catch Sebastian's eye and I'm surprised to see tears in them. Did he really care about Ray that much?

Tannini talks about his early memories of my father and how close they became as friends and the funny times they had while fishing at the lake and camping in the woods. There are a few polite chuckles from people, but I'm distracted. Just behind Sebastian, in the distance, just out of view is female figure dressed all in black with a heavy laced veil covering her face and hair. I turn towards Jono and whisper: 'Do you know who that is?'

Jono follows my eye line and shakes his head. 'Probably someone who was helped by Ray.'

He's probably right, but there's something about her that makes me uneasy and unable to concentrate on what Tannini is saying. Even though I can't see, I'm sure she's staring right back at me too and it's not feeling good.

'Ignore her. Pay attention,' Jono hisses at me.

It's then I realise that the angel and Tannini are waiting for something from me and it takes a moment for me to remember. I'm supposed to say something too. Getting to my feet, I negotiate heels and grass so I don't fall face first. As I pass the coffin a sudden thought enters my head. What if I trip and knock the coffin over? What if I do that and there's nothing inside? Shaking the thought away, I stand beside Tannini, who gives me a small hug. It is now I can see who has followed us to the willow tree. The whole town has come to say goodbye and to make it worse they are all looking at me.

Digging into my pocket, I pull out the piece of paper that I've scribbled on and start to speak, but nothing comes out. The words are stuck in my throat; my tongue feels thick and swollen in my mouth. Glancing at Tannini, he gives me a nod, but still can't.

'Don't be scared?' he whispers.

I nod and start to read off the paper. I'm not talking to the crowd, I'm reading. If I look up then I'll lose my nerve and I just have to get this over with, even if I do sound robotic. When I'm done, with my head still lowered, I hurry back to my seat.

'Now we must prepare to commit our brother Ray Marley into the ground where his body will become at one with the gift our father gave us,' Simiel says.

But then something truly astounding happens and it causes my resolve to break. Candice moves to the front of crowd and looking at her, I know that Lorreli has control. Standing stock still, she opens her mouth and the most beautiful noise comes out as she starts to sing. I've no idea what the words are, but she sounds like…well she sounds like an angel. Then Uz steps forward and joins in with a deep bass voice that melds into Lorreli's perfectly. Finally Micka also starts to sing with a soft tenor tone and it sends shivers down my spine.

Simiel scowls their way, but it doesn't stop them. I think he knows that he's no power over them. He must be one of the lower angels, but give him his dues, he merely stands with his eyes to the ground as we all listen.

At first I've no idea what they are trying to do, until the brightest light starts to emerge from the ground. It grows bigger and brighter and I start to notice small figures within. There's a collective gasp from behind and Danny whispers that these must be angels. I can barely comprehend what he's just said, because I'm on my knees in shock, tears falling hard and fast down my cheeks. Both Danny and Jono are beside me holding me against them. The angels gather around my father's coffin and then that same white light starts to emerge from the coffin and it takes a moment for me to realise what was happening. They were taking father's soul back home.

When it was all over and the light disappeared, there was a silence and with a small nod from the angel, the coffin is lowered into the ground and I say my final goodbye.

The walk back to the Mina's is a slow one and Uz catches up to me and pulls me a little away from the walking crowd.

'I didn't know that was going to happen I swear,' he says.

'I'm not mad, Uz. I'm just surprised. Why did they take him?'

'I've no idea. I only knew they would when Lorreli started to sing and that instinct kicked in. The Choirs made that decision and took him where he belongs.'

'But I thought the Powers forbid it?' I ask.

'The Choirs have their own laws. If they chose to take Ray, then they will take him no matter what. His spirit is where it belongs and at peace.'

'Will I ever understand your world?' I say.

Uz gives me a small smile as he shakes his head. Of course I'll never understand it, because even the angels don't understand it. They just exist.

Finally, we get to Mina's and I see the effort the Roses have gone to. Sandwiches, cakes and other buffet foods lay on the tables. On the bar is a picture of my father and beside it his favourite drink, white rum.

Everyone is mingling politely and eating and drinking. I feel exhausted, but I know, I've just got to get through this final part before hiding back within my four walls.

'I'd hoped I would be the one walking by your side today.'

I sigh deeply as Sebastian comes to my side. I'm not in the mood and I really wish he knew me enough to know this. Even Micka has not come anywhere near me. He's remained to the other side of the room.

'I had my family with me,' I answer.

'I should have been at your side. You made me look a fool.'

I turn towards him. 'Don't do this now.'

'Mina, I've no idea what more you want me to do?'

'I want you to give me time to grieve and get through this day. As my future husband it's not a lot to ask.'

'Even more reason for me to be by your side,' he pushes.

I start to walk away from him, but he grabs me by the arm and pulls me to him. People are looking, I don't have to look to know this, so I allow it, wrapping my arms around his neck and kissing his cheek.

'I'm not Eve, I will not be commanded by anyone,' I whisper.

Hurt and anger flares in Sebastian's eyes, but continues to hold me.

'No, you are nothing like Eve, she loved me unconditionally,' he hisses. 'But I've never given you any reason to believe I hold you down.'

I'm behaving unfairly and I know he's right, but I'm just defensive at the moment and need some space. Is it too much to ask for? Sebastian has no other choice but to allow me to leave his side. His weakness is being shown up in public and I'm exploiting that fact unashamedly. I search for Jaq and find her near the bar area, serving tea and coffee.

'Let me help,' I say grabbing a coffee pot.

Freda grabs the pot off me with a look that makes me shrink away.

'You will not,' she snaps. 'This is our job.'

'I just wanted to talk to Jaq,' I say.

'Marianne,' she calls.

Jaq's older sister comes towards us and Freda gives her the jug and nudges Jaq and I away from the counter.

'What happened at the funeral with the angels?' she asks as we sit down together.

'Uz, says that the Choir of angels took him.'

'And how do you feel about that?' she asks.

I shrug, because I've no idea what else to say. It feels good just being relaxed in her company once more. There's something different about her, that I only notice today. She seems fuller in the face and slightly more flushed than usual. I've no idea what her mother's feeding her, but it must be doing her good, because she looks great. Just wish I looked as refreshed.

'Sebastian seems a little edgy,' she says after a moment.

'He's not happy with me, but I suppose I'm not helping things either. Look, after everyone's gone, will you stay back. I feel we really need to catch up. I miss having you around.'

A smile warms her face even more as she nods, just as Freda calls her name. Two hours later, with a diner fully cleaned down, I finally manage to get Freda out of the door, Jaq and I are huddled up on my sofa nursing glasses of wine.

It feels good with just the two of us. Life this past year has really stretched our friendship to the point of breaking. We've not really spoken much after my return and Jaq's walking out of Mina's. There's nothing really to say after that. But I have missed our closeness and hearing news of her days. So I start by asking her about Dom, but she evades the question with another directly at me.

'I don't know what to say,' I answer.

'Well just tell me what happened when you went to the city with Micka. Why all of a sudden did you end up at Sebastian's?'

'If I tell you then it must stay between us. I've not even told Jono.'

She nods and I tell her all what happens the night of my birthday and the ultimatum Gabriel left me. This shocks her.

'Gabriel? As in dress up in the nativity Gabriel?' she asks.

'We've never done nativity here. This is Supton,' I laugh.

'I know, but I know someone who talked about it when I was visiting Carla.'

'Well then yes the very same, but don't expect tinsel halo and tacky wings,' I say with a smirk.

'From what you've already said he sounds like a cock.'

'Let me finish,' I say.

I then proceed to tell her all about the Marley bloodline and that being the Primum means I'm the incarnation of the first woman. To my surprise she merely nods and there's not a flicker of surprise from her. This should have rocked her like it did me, but it hasn't.

'You already know this?'

Jaq nods: 'I only know because Ray told me in order to help you when you were not being yourself. But I didn't know about Gabriel. So you really are Lilith?'

'No I'm Mina, just a little part of her lives on in me. Like a legacy.'

'And Sebastian…?'

'Is Adam.'

'Wow! Dare I ask about Micka?'

I shrug because I don't know what to say. Throughout this whole thing, he's respectively kept his distance. That's what I miss and realise. He has hardly ever pushed his presence on me and that's the reason I should not compare him to Sebastian. They both are men in their own right, but love and care for me in their own way. Sebastian is overwhelming with showering his love and affection on me and sometimes I need that to curb my insecurities, but then when I'm standing free and on my own, I need Micka to just stand in the background just in case. He trusts that I will make the right decision first.

'You can at least tell me if you're still in love with him?' she pushes.

I smile. 'Yes, but I can't have him. I can never have him. Anyway, what about you? Is there any gossip?'

I frown as a flinch passes through her. Something is going on, but she doesn't want to say. I want to push her but we are interrupted by my phone ringing.

'Hello?'

Silence—I glance at the screen and see that the number is withheld.

'Hello?' I try again, still nothing.

'Look you sick bastards just fuck off,' I snap before disconnecting.

'What's that?' Jaq asks.

'The Emandato have stooped to pervy phonecalls,' I say. 'Where were we?'

Jaq gets to her feet and tugs on her jacket.

'I've got to go. I promised mum I'd help her out.'

'Could you not stay?' I ask.

Jaq gives me a squeeze. 'I'm really sorry. Maybe another night.'

There's no choice but to let her go and leave me alone. I stand the silence for at least half an hour before grabbing my coat and getting in the car. Before I can even blink, I'm opening the door of my father's house and standing in the hallway. There's no warmth here no more and I wonder what I'll do with it now. This house and the Manor are both Marley homes, but I can't have both, not when it should really go to Danny.

That's it. My mind made up. I'm going to give the house to Danny.

Tannini's Journal 15th July 0230hrs

I walked into my house after the longest day and poured myself another stiff drink. I'd already drunk far too much at the wake, but I just needed something to numb the pain.

Seeing Mina at the graveside broke my heart. She should never have been there so young. She held herself with so much strength until the angels appeared. Uz called them the Choirs. I've heard rumours about this band of angels. They are a little like the Militants. A law onto themselves, but they are not as bound by obedience like the Militants and Gabriel is their leader so to speak. I'm pretty sure he had a hand in it.

The Choirs are notorious for overriding the rule of the Powers. The souls they take become like them, whether it be human, or Other and there is no steadfast rule of why they chose them. All angels work best to music, but it is said that when the war between Lucifer and the Powers. A small band of angels remained and sang a lament in doing so caused the greatest rainfall Earth had ever had. The Powers tried to stop them, but nothing could, until the angel's great father come forth. He offered to not condemn all of Lucifer's followers and if they could get them to repent then they could re-join the fold. And so the Choirs were created.

Going to the cupboards, I need to eat, but drink seems to be doing the job better, plus there's a need for a shower.

Then there's a knock at my door, frowning, I check the time. Beverley would not risk coming over just yet. Going to the door, I find a young girl of around seventeen standing there. I look at her puzzled for a moment.

'Can I help?' I say finally.

'Stan Tannini?' she asks.

My defences automatically go up as I look at this slip of a girl.

'Who's asking?'

'I'm Sammy Clayton.'

'As in Gi-Gi—I mean Gina Clayton?'

She nods. A sudden sense of dread flows over me. I've not seen or heard from Gi-Gi in nearly eighteen years.

'Yes, I'm her daughter.'

'Why are you here?'

'Can we do this inside?' she asks.

'Look, I'm not trying to be funny, but this is not a good time. Why don't you just tell me what you want and then you can go back to your mother.'

A look of pain flashes across her face and the dread sinks further.

'My mother died a month ago. I've come here, because she told me that you're my father.'

She may as well punch me clean in the face as I tell her that's impossible.

'Look can I come in? I'm freezing my arse off out here.'

'Not before you prove that you are who you say you are.'

Sighing, she gives me a roll of her eyes and I briefly see Gi-Gi in her face.

'Mum was human and if she was human then how can I do this.'

And she turns right there and then. In front of me. The owl looks at me with wide dark eyes and my body is shaking.

'Please change back and then you'd better come in once you're dressed.'

I turn my back on her as I hear her change. Once we are in my front room, I try and take her in. See if

I can see any family resemblance. She has Gi-Gi's fair hair and round face, but her eyes remind me of my mothers. Brightest blue and piercing. The jeans and t-shirt are clean and tidy. The front emblazoned with a faded band logo of a mouth with its tongue hanging out.

'Is the owl your core?' I ask.

'Yes.'

'That doesn't prove anything.'

She smiles. 'Mum didn't know about you. You never told her. She only found out when I was born because I changed in the cot. She then did some research and found out about this town and you.'

I've nothing else to say, because deep down I can see the truth. I never told Gi-Gi about what I was. But finding out I've a daughter is a blow to the system. Children were never supposed to happen, yet, I feel sad that I missed out on this one growing up.

'So what do you want? I take it your mother made sure you were taken care of?'

'She did, so don't worry I'm not here to ask for money,' she snaps.

I've crossed the line and insulted her already and she's only been here a few minutes. I thought all my years around Mina and Jaq would give me some idea, but it's clear I don't and nerves are setting in and controlling my tongue.

'Forgive me. It's been a long day.'

'You were at that funeral. Was it someone important?'

'My best friend. Look, what made you come here?'

She sits down and sighs. 'I just wanted to meet you. Mum spoke so highly of you and from what I've heard from others you're a good man. I don't need your money or anything. I just wanted to see you for myself.'

My hearts starts to soften and after offering her a drink, we sit together and talk. She tells me that her mother had sought the help when Sammy had first turned and met with a man called Torsten, who became almost like an uncle to her. He taught her through the years how to use and control her gift and then suggested that she register with the Council. He of course had claimed parentage, because Gi-Gi had begged not to involve me. She felt that I deserved to get on with my life without the complication. As for Sammy, she's now at college and wants to train animals.

She accepts my offer to stay in the spare room and now I'm sitting up writing this, because there is so much shit going through my head. With the Council watching my every move they are going to get curious. It's an offence to deceive them and claim a child is your own if not. Both myself and Sammy could get punished. They know I've no siblings, so I have no idea how I'm going to hide her from them and save us both. Maybe I should contact them directly and just own up.

Robratto

Jaq's Email to Carla 25th July 1025hrs

I've done it. I couldn't take the guessing anymore. The blue line looks and mocks me with its result. I didn't really need to take it. I knew deep inside that I was pregnant, but now I'm at a loss to know what to do. How am I going to explain this to everyone? How am I even going to explain this to Dom? There are choices for me, I know that, but I need guidance. Can I come over to yours? Just for a little while.

Let me know.

Much Love

Jaq

Candice's Journal 25th July 1030hrs

Morag has returned to me with news from the King and Queen. Apparently, they have heard a rumour about who fronts this Emandato. They wish me to warn the angels and work with them. They are keen on keeping Mina safe.

So now, I'm in my front room with both Morag and Gabriel and it's like a fucking fridgebox in here. After their earlier confrontation this is going to be interesting. But they need to work together in this.

'So what is this rumour?' Gabriel snaps.

It's obvious by the smug look on Morag's face that she's enjoying having one up on the angel. I don't mind admitting it rocks my boat too. He's a little jumped up and with red hair like that he's not really got anything to strut around for.

'My King and Queen want to know what you will do with the information when we give it to you?'

Gabriel huffs, frustration on his face. He's getting pissed off and I'm forcing the grin off my face.

'What are they expecting me to do?' he snarls.

'They want an intervention. They know what happens when angels should be punished. They get a lot of sway when it comes to the Powers. You yourself cannot deny that fact.'

Fuck me, that Fae has some guts, she's just insulted one of the highest order of angels and isn't even batting an eyelid.

'I know what you're trying to do. This is because of this foolish notion of your so called Great Mother. Get it into your thick skull she will not return,' he hisses.

'How can you be so sure,' Morag pushes.

'She will not return,' he snarls.

'But you don't know that. Our signs suggest...'

'They suggest nothing, Fae.'

'We know more about your sister than you. She is our Great Mother. The first of our race.'

'Don't make me laugh,' he mocks, but I can tell he's getting twitchy.

'Our Great Mother is returning to us in all her glory and you're lying, because you know it too.'

'I am not lying, she will not return.'

'And pray tell how you can be so sure,' Morag throws.

'Because she never left you, you stupid bitch.'

We both look at him shocked and Lorreli's sudden *oh shit!* Startles me. I think he's just as fucking shocked, because it's something I'm sure wasn't supposed to be known.

'What do you mean she never left?' Morag whispers.

'Please tell me what you know about the Emandato,' Gabriel almost begs. 'And once I know I'll kill them myself.'

'Even if it's one of your own brothers?'

Gabriel almost steps back as though she's punched him.

'I need to speak to Candice on her own,' he snaps.

'I forbid it,' Morag argues.

'Get out!' he booms and looking at me, she scuttles from the room.

Now, I'm fucking scared and alone with a pissed off archangel.

'Get Lorreli,' he snaps.

'I'm not letting her take over me, so you can have an angelic pow wow,' I answer.

He takes a deep breath to steady himself and his tone changes.

'Candice, sweetheart, I want you here too. Just get Lorreli. Is she with you?'

Lorreli is already there, I can feel her and she reassures me everything will be fine, so I nod.

'Great, now I want to know what she thinks about my brother.'

I start to relay the question, but then realise like the idiot I am she can hear everything. She takes her time in answering and when she does I give Gabriel my answer.

'She thinks you know the answer deep down. He's capable of anything and Mina goes against all that is pure.'

'But I can't defeat him,' Gabriel says. 'He is much stronger and very much favoured by the Powers.'

'But if she dies before her legacy can be brought forward then the Powers have bigger problems on their hands.'

Gabriel falls silent for a moment and I can't help but feel sorry for the guy. It's like the wind's been truly knocked out of him.

'Dare I ask which brother it is?' I say.

He looks up me with a resigned expression on his face.

'Do you really want to know?' he asks.

I nod and he sighs. 'The brother who your people think is wanting Mina dead is Michael and if that is indeed true then you and I are all in deep shit.'

Tannini's Journal 25th July 0230hrs.

It's strange having a teenage girl in the house. I'm having to painfully aware of knocking every time I change rooms in my own home. She seems pliable enough and very polite. She doesn't want to step on my toes or anything and seems willing to get to know me.

I've told her about my upbringing and about the Tannini family. Showed her pictures etc. I'm not sure what else to do, but she seems content with just that. Her own stories about her mother and growing up settle my nerves about her. This Torsten really did do right by them both.

I've decided to take the bull by the horns and go to see The Council. If I make the first move then they may be lenient towards us. Of course Sammy is nervous. She knows as well as I do their reputation, but I've promised we'll do this together.

However, there's another problem that's getting in my way. Laura Roberts has been found and being held by one of my colleagues in the city. Apparently, she was found living in one of the top hotels and the manager was suspicious of the amount of different men that came and went. So later, I will be making my way to the city to check her out.

Mina's Online Blog 25th July 2345hrs

'I can't take the house, Mina. It's yours.'

Danny is still arguing with me about the blasted house.

'Why? It's yours by right. I have the Manor. Both are Marley properties,' I argue back.

'You grew up in that home. It's what's left of your mother and father.'

'Please Uncle Danny. I can't live in that house and neither can I sell it. Just live in it for me and if it makes you feel better pay rent.'

Danny reluctantly agrees and we shake on some nominal monthly rent figure, which he doesn't realise will go straight back to him. I'm a Marley and we are sneaky fuckers.

'How's everything else?' he asks.

I shrug my answer.

'Come on Mina, tell me. Has there been any more freezing bath episodes?'

'Not since Marleux. I'm still not sure what happened and why he made a difference.'

'You mean you don't understand why Uzrel was in that room with you and what it meant?' Danny asks.

I flinch at Uz's name and the memory of us locked in that basement. I've tried not to think about it since and I'm sure the same goes for Uz. I was a ball of so much sexual energy and cooped up in that small space with pure source was too much. I tortured him and seduced him.

We never had full sex, but I still toyed with him, played with him. Showed him the sexual pleasures a human woman could give. Then beat him violently when the rages took over. I abused him beyond any level and Gabriel allowed it to happen. Keeping him docile to appease me.

'I only know that it worked,' I answer.

'With Uzrel as the heaven and Marleux as hell, in one room you were able to supercharge your polar opposites and channel them through your father's. Hence why you now feel normal.'

It seems to make some sense now, but it was a big risk to take when they had no idea if it's work.

'I'm fine now,' I reassure. 'Nothing has happened since.'

'And how's things with Sebastian?'

'I'm not sure. Things are tense and all the stress is causing me to feel unwell.'

'Well that's understandable. Just take it easy now.'

The sound of my phone interrupts us. Pulling it out, I see that it's Tannini. He tells me about Laura and I practically run from Danny's to the station where Tannini waits. I must look frightful as I hurtle through the front doors, because he takes a step back from me.

'Mina, what the fuck?'

'Where is she?' I demand.

'I'll take you to her. She's downstairs.'

I know where he means. The special place where Dom was housed. He takes me through the station and down the stairs to those cells. Anger flows through me every step I take. This little bitch is the reason that my father is rotting in the ground. There are no words that can describe what I want to do to her. The pain I wish her to feel. Tannini must feel it, because he keeps looking over at me as we walk. Finally, we reach the last cell of the block and Tannini stops.

'What?' I ask.

'Before you go in, know that there's no paperwork for her. She's not here.'

'Which means?'

'Which means whatever happens in there stays in there.'

The meaning is clear. I'm free to act on any feeling that I have. I have the blessing of the law and there's nothing that Laura can do about it.

'Mina, I've placed her in a seal so she's useless,' he says.

'I want you to lift it.'

'Mina…'

'Stan, lift it. I will face her as an equal.'

He nods and pushes a button on the side of the cell.

'Any trouble, I will be in there,' he says.

He steps away and leaves me to turn towards the locked cell door. Laura looks up at me and holds a smug look on her face. She knows the power is down and she's free to do her worst. Opening the door, I lock us both in and throw the key towards Tannini. Only one of us is leaving this room and I intend it to be me. She looks less polished and a little ruffled. She's wearing jeans and black t shirt with her hair tied up. Not a scrap of make-up on, but still, she's beautiful. Charm oozing off her.

'Wondered how long it would take for Supton's princess to grace me with her presence,' she mocks.

'I think the term you are looking for is queen,' I answer.

A broad smile spreads on her face and I feel nervous butterflies in my stomach.

'No, I meant what I said, because the real queen has returned.'

I've no idea what she means and I don't want to give the satisfaction of asking, so it's ignored.

'So where is your father?' I ask.

'I've no idea,' she answers.

'Funny that.'

'What about yours? In hell I suppose. Oh! And one in heaven, so I hear?'

My fist hurts as I pull it back from her face. Blood spills onto her clothes and satisfaction is mine to hold.

'What happened to being in protective custody?' she tries to laugh, but it comes out choked.

'It doesn't apply in this place,' I say.

'Do your worst then bitch.'

Every ounce of anger and resentment bubbles to the surface and the rising feeling of power I got when Danny pushed me into the prison is there again. But I'm not going to just explode. She's going to suffer slowly. With the help of the elements, I make her heat up first. Shifting the temperature a little higher. I can feel the power of every living thing running through my body in pulses and I focus on the effect I need. She of course can do the same, but she's no angel and I have the edge. I've always had the edge.

She squeals and cries, but doesn't seem to break, but tries to fight back. The cell is now an ice-block as I freeze her now, but still I'm not done.

Then just as quick the elements change and the cell becomes a wind tunnel as it lifts me from my feet and causes me to hit the wall. Good, she's fighting back. The rain is the next thing to fall as she sends me flying across the room once more, but with my adrenaline high, I turn the rain into hail and force them to fall hard and fast. Yes, it's hurting me too, but right now I don't give a damn.

'You think you've got it made,' she screams. 'You're going to die one way or another. They can't let you live.'

'I will live and nothing your little group can do will change that fact.'

'It's nothing to do with the Emandato you stupid bitch. The Powers want you dead too. They hate you.'

'Then I'll just see you on the other side.'

I want her dead. I want to rip her limb from limb and that's what I do. Closing my eyes, I reach down deep and pull on all the darkness of hell and finish her.

When I come back from that dark place, I'm shocked by what I see. Blood and body parts cover the room, even my clothes. I look down at my blood stained hands and surprised that I don't feel remorse. Turning slowly, I make way out of the cell and see Tannini's pale face looking at me.

'I'm afraid I've made a bit of mess,' I say.

'Fucking hell Mina, that's an understatement. Did you get anything out of her?'

He pokes his head into the room and he starts to gag at the sight.

'Was I supposed to?' I ask.

'This is going to take some explaining. Yes, Mina I needed to know who the leader is?' he snaps.

I start to argue back when with a small breeze, Gabriel appears in the corridor.

'How the fuck did you manage to get down here?' Tannini stutters.

'Your spells don't mean anything to me,' Gabriel snaps. 'Where is the Roberts girl?'

Painfully aware of the state I'm in and Gabriel's frown, I now realise that I may have been a little hasty.

'Mina, why are you covered in blood?' he asks in a slow deliberate way that causes me to shrink towards Tannini.

He pushes past me and I hear him cuss as he takes in the state of the cell.

'You stupid little child,' he shouts.

Grabbing my arm, he pulls me towards him. He's beyond furious, but in my fear, I cause a rain storm right there in the corridor.

'She killed my father,' I whimper.

'And she was under the protection of the Archangel Michael, my brother. If you wanted a war with heaven then you are going to well and truly get one.'

'Well I didn't ask for it and anyway according to her the your people want me just as dead,' I mutter.

'Believe me if I wanted you dead you would be by now.'

Gabriel pulls me further to him as though he's just going to zap us both out, when something stops him. Looking deep into my eyes, his breath catches.

'Mr Tannini, your council told you everything I assume,' Gabriel says without taking his eyes off me.

'Yes sir,' he answers.

'Then you best tell them that the game has changed. The deal has been sealed and we in Supton need protection.'

Tannini gives me a second glance, before running off back upstairs.

'What does that mean?' I ask.

'You have a wedding to arrange. You must marry Sebastian by the end of next month.'

'But I…'

'Mina, do as I say. Marry your soul mate and become one, because from this moment you are going to need all the protection you can get.

·

Robratto PT 2

Tannini's Jounral 27th July 0230hrs

As soon as Gabriel told me the news I got in the car with Sammy and took us both to where some of the Council was staying just outside Supton.

In the car with Sammy, I told her that we would tell them that I'm her father and admit the deceit.

'They may be forgiving,' I say. 'Especially since I have other news.'

'What's that?' she asks.

I look at her briefly.

'What do you know about Supton or the Marleys?'

'Oooh I know of Jono Marley. Do you know him? He lives in Supton doesn't he?'

In that moment, I see a young woman fresh out of her teens and it's endearing. However, the fact that my new found daughter has a crush on Jono Marley, whether it be from a far or not, is unsettling.

'Yes he does, but he's not a guy to be messing with,' I say.

I get a wry smirk from her. I've already stepped into protective dad and it amuses her.

'Well I'd just want an autograph anyway,' she answers. 'So what's so important about the Marleys?'

The car journey is just long enough for me to explain who Mina is and why the interest from the Council. She still looks shell-shocked as we park the car outside the small cottage.

'Are you okay to go in?' I ask.

She nods and we both get out of the car and make our way to the stone cottage. It's all really quant and pretentious, but I shouldn't be surprised.

The members of the Council here are Sophia, Christopher and Oscar. I barely know them, but I've heard Beverley talk about Oscar and Sophia. They are brother and sister and a little highly strung. Her words not mine. I'd use jumped up pompous dicks with too much money.

We are greeted at the door by a Heavy and then ushered inside. The cottage is fairly large and in the front room sits the three of them. Sophia wears a long maxi dress that curls round her body where she sits. Her long brown hair loose, she's beautiful there's no denying that and Oscar is no different. His slender body fits well in white linen shirt and trousers. Christopher, however, looks very much like the father. A little stocky and tired looking, I suspect that living with the precious pair can be draining.

Sammy has moved closer to me. To a newbie these people are intimidating and I feel sorry for her.

'What do we owe this pleasure?' Oscar asks.

'Oscar, dearest, don't forget your manners. At least offer Mr Tannini and his young daughter refreshment,' Sophia says silkily. 'Jeffery, fetch some cold lemonade.'

Another gentleman who I'd not noticed until he moved, left the room. The shock of her calling Sammy my daughter must be evident, because Sophia looks suitably smug.

'Do you really think we would not know?' she says. 'We of course have helped Samantha find her way to you.'

I glance quickly at Sammy and see puzzlement on her face.

'Do not fret. The young one had no idea. You realise that it is punishable to lie about a child's parentage?' Oscar added.

'Yes, sir, but both Sammy and I are not to blame for Torsten's actions.'

It feels odd calling a jumped up little prick sir, but neither am I suicidal. These three are the most powerful on the Council. They pull the strings in effect, because they have the money.

'I agree,' Sophia says.

Jeffery returns with glasses of iced lemonade and places it on the table before handing each one of us a glass. I don't like lemonade, but my mouth is so dry from anxiety that I have to drink something.

'We will allow this misdemeanour pass because you've been so helpful with the Marley situation. However, we would like Samantha to reregister with us correctly and become a fully-fledged part of the Council,' she continues.

Panic fills my chest. Why would they want my daughter to be part of the Council? Why not just leave her be?

'What does that mean?' Sammy asks.

'It means Samantha that you will join the ranks of the Council. You will be trained and employed by us,' Sophia says.

'But I'm going to train with animals. Maybe open my own sanctuary,' Sammy says.

'You will honour the gift we are offering,' Oscar snaps.

Sammy flinches and stands closer to me. Opening my mouth, I start to defend her but its Christopher that speaks.

'Oscar, curb that temper. Samantha should be admired for trying to make a life for herself and it is a good cause.'

'Yes, but she should do what was promised,' Oscar throws.

'And what about her free will? Are we now just like those Powers that Be?' Christopher asks.

'That is not what my brother is saying,' Sophia argues.

The tension in the room is fucking tight and reaching out, I take Sammy's hand. She gives me a slight nod. If this kicks off then we are shifting and getting out of here. Getting between a Council heated debate is not my idea of fun. Things can get nasty.

'Silence!' Christopher suddenly snaps and the brother and sister stop. 'Now young lady may I apologise for my members here bad manners. They have shown us up and shown you disrespect. Mr Tannini, you may or may not know this, but your daughter is a very special individual.' I turn towards Sammy and she gives a slow nod.

'Yes,' she whispers.

'What sort of gift?' I ask.

'When we as shifters change into our animal, we are still human in our consciousness and so cannot commune with any beast. Yet, Sammy here can do it and with some ease. When she changes she fully becomes that animal, hence the career choice I hasten to add,' Christopher says.

'Really? You can do that?' I ask.

Pride fills me. What she can do is a great gift and a very good reason why the Council want her. It's rare for a Shifter to shift completely like that.

'Yes and I still have that gift when I'm in my human state. It's weaker, but still there. I just want to use it for good,' she says.

'Of course you do,' Christopher says. 'And I am willing to help you achieve that dream. I will offer you my backing.'

'And what do you want in return?' I ask.

'Her loyalty. She has a gift we could use,' he answers. 'Look, Mr Tannini, I understand your concern. I will personally sponsor Samantha and support her and all she has to do is help us when it comes to those shifters that have problems returning to their human form.'

I'd heard of those shifters. They would become obsessed with their core animal and spend months in that state and so losing their humanity. Stuck in a world of neither animal nor human. It's a fucked up state of being, but it happens. The Council take them in and try and rehabilitate them or rumour has it have them killed if they are a lost cause.

'Can I think about it?' Sammy asks.

I nearly choke when Christopher agrees. They are not usually so amiable.

'Come back to us after you have finished your education and we will discuss it then. In the meantime you will be registered at the Council as Samantha Tannini and you will use it. Agreed?'

'She doesn't need to…' I start.

'I agree,' Sammy says.

'Then that is settled. Welcome Samantha Tannini to the Council family,' Christopher smiles. 'Now, Mr Tannini, you have something more to tell us.'

After taking a mouthful of lemonade, I pass on the message given by Gabriel. All of a sudden, Oscar and Sophia's attitude warms towards us.

Once Sammy and I are in my car, we both breathe a sigh of relief. That was the most intense experience in my life.

'Are you okay?' I ask.

Sammy nods. 'I'm sorry if I dragged you into something,' she says.

'Don't be stupid,' I chastise. 'You are a Tannini now and I was already in this mess long before you were ever born.'

I decide to drive her home to the city. It's not safe for her to be with me at the moment in Supton. There's too much shit going on and I don't want her getting in the way and hurt. Sammy doesn't even argue, because she knows deep down that being near me at the moment is not good. Supton is no place to be for any Otherworldly.

As soon as I say goodbye to Sammy, I get another phone call. Robratto is in Supton demanding Laura.

Fucking great! That's all I need.

Candice's Journal 27th July 2245hrs

First thing that happens is Gabriel with a blood stained Mina on my doorstep. He pushes her towards the bathroom and tells her to get showered.

'You'll need to lend her some clothes,' he says.

'Maybe you could tell me what the fuck is going on?' I snap.

'She murdered the Roberts girl.'

'What do you mean by murdered?'

'I mean ripped her in two murdered. That girl is pieces and now I've heard that her forefather is demanding her back.'

And then he's gone. Left me alone with a psychotic angelicdemon. I can't believe that fucking angel has dumped her on me. What am I supposed to do?

'Keep her safe here. She needs you,' Lorreli says.

'I think I'm the one that needs protecting,' I mutter.

Going to my bedroom, I try and find something plain that will fit Mina, settling on some jeans and a vest top I leave them on the bed.

'Mina, I've left some more clothes on the bed,' I say through the bathroom door.

'Cheers.'

Is all I hear and decide to leave her alone for a bit. Well to be honest, I don't want to be pissing her off any time soon. I remember finding out about the heaven and hell inside her. I didn't realise this would be the result.

'What if she wants to leave?' I ask.

'Remember what you can do,' Lorreli reminds me. 'But there's something else...'

The door opening with a fully dressed Mina interrupts her.

'You look like you could do with a drink. I've some Jack.'

Mina smiles and gives me a nod.

'I'd kill for one.'

I stiffen at her comment and she notices.

'Sorry bad choice of words,' she mutters.

'Hey, I'm not here to judge. Fuck, I'd probably done the same thing,' I say.

This gets a much bigger smile from her and her stance relaxes a little. I've not known Mina for long, but to kill someone is not in her nature. This must be pulling at every moral fibre inside her head. As a human and angel. The demon won't care. Revenge fed that side of her. I hand her the glass and she downs it in one only to convulse and throw it back up in the kitchen sink.

'That's the shock,' I offer. 'When you pull someone to bits that tends to happen so I'm told.'

She grabs a towel and wipes her face.

'I suppose,' she whispers. 'I never meant to. She just pissed me off and I wanted her to hurt in all the ways I'd hurt.'

'How do you feel now?'

'Like shit,' she smirks. 'Do you mind if I go and lie down?'

I tell her to go into Nanna's bed and wait until she's out of earshot before shouting Uz's name. I don't know, why I'm calling Mina's godfather, but he and I have developed some form of friendship. We help each other and I think he uses my connection to Lorreli to help. Since Mina's incident, he's become even more withdrawn and reliant of Lorreli and myself. Although I've no idea what has caused it.

'I can't be here.'

His voice causes me to quickly close us into a room. I don't want Mina knowing I'm using him.

'What's happening with Robratto?'

'He's holding Jono as ransom…'

'I thought he'd gone back to the city.'

Uz shrugs. 'He kidnapped him. Where's Mina?'

'She's gone up for a nap.'

And he's gone and then back again in a flash.

'You could use the stairs,' I start to say, before I realise that he's as white as a sheet.

'You know I was only kidding about the stairs.'

Grabbing my arm, he grips me tightly.

'Mina's not up there. I'm going to need you with me.'

'I'm not going anywhere,' is all I get out before we are both in the centre of town. It takes a moment of a headrush and sickness before I find my feet. But the ground won't stop moving and I realise it's not me.

Supton's town centre is shaking from an earthquake, which I suspect is Mina's doing. I can't see her, but Robratto has his hands round Jono's neck, who is on his knees. There's pure fury on Robratto's face.

'Where is my daughter?' he's screams.

Danny is trying his best to get to them but whatever Robratto is doing its stopping anyone getting through.

'You hurt my son and I swear on Lucifer himself I'll drag you to hell myself you son of a bitch,' he screams.

A car comes to a screeching halt and Mr Daniels runs from the car towards me.

'Where's Mina?' he demands.

'She's escaped from mine,' I say.

'What do you mean by escape,' he asks through gritted teeth.

'She must have heard about Jono,' Uz steps up. 'You know the bond she has with her cousin.'

Mr Daniels takes a step back like he's been punched.

'What do you mean by that?' he whispers.

I've no idea what the fuck Uz has said, but it's clearly hit a nerve with Mr Daniels.

'I mean that if Mina tore that Roberts girl in two for her father, what she going to do if Jonathan dies. All the work with Marleux will be over, we will lose Mina forever if she kills anyone else.'

'And how do you suppose we are going to stop her?' Mr Daniels asks.

Uz places a hand on my shoulder and I see disbelief on Mr Daniels' face.

'She is Fae.'

'She is Mina's equal.'

'Where is that bitch succubus?' Robratto shouts.

'She is not here,' Mr Daniels shouts. 'Maybe you should deal with me instead.'

Robratto laughs. 'Deal with the likes of you. I don't talk to the monkey. Now where is she?'

Mr Daniels turns towards Uz and tells him to find Mina. The angel disappears.

The afternoon sun starts to lower as the stand-off continues. No one can get near Jono, due to the magick that surrounds them both. We've had Faes try and break through. Even the Weres and Shifters has had a go, but that Robratto bastard is holding strong. Poor Mr. Marley looks beyond himself. There in front of him is his son who could die at any given moment, and there's nothing we can do about it.

Some of the town have scuttled back to their homes. A little afraid now of getting involved further and there's still no sign of Mina.

'What is taking him so long? Surely she can't be that hard to find,' Mr Daniels mutters.

'Well maybe you asked the wrong angel?' I say.

Mr Daniels turns on me in a flash: 'Your meaning?'

'My meaning is that Gabriel may have more power in tracking her down.'

I watch as he visibly calms down. I'd already seen Micka circling trying to do his thing, no doubt knowing if he makes a move he could kill them both. Obviously, Mr Daniels hadn't noticed, but it's fucking fun to watch him squirm. I am just about to say something else when something happens that turns my stomach.

It's on the floor before I realise what has flown over our heads. It lands with a sickening thud that I'm sure I'm going to puke. There's a deafening silence that follows as Robratto takes in the sight of Laura's bloodied head before him. Mina strolls from behind and stands beside it. Uz suddenly appears at my side and steps within my space. Touching a little too closely.

'I've brought you Laura, now give me my cousin.'

'Candice, make sure you are ready,' Uz whispers.

'What do you want me to do?' I ask.

'You will know. The demon must not die by her hand.'

The ground beneath us shakes violently and everyone takes a step back.

'You will pay. A head for a head, you Marley bitch,' Robratto hisses.

His grip on Jono's head tightens and I wait to hear the snap of bone. Then, Lorreli suddenly takes me over and words I've never heard come out my mouth just as Mina is running towards Robratto. Understanding, Uz flies towards Mina and in the brightest of white flashes, they've both gone. Jono is covered in blood and it takes me moment to realise that it's not his. At my feet, is the gutted body of Robratto and my hands are shaking.

'Candice, you need to breathe,' I hear Lorreli say. 'Your hands are clean. I killed him.'

'Where's Mina?' Sebastian shouts.

'Tell him I sent her somewhere safe,' she says.

I relay the message and his face reddens.

'And where exactly is that?' he hisses.

'The safest place any angel can be, home,' she answers. 'Now you get Jonathan out of here and cleaned up.'

Mr Marley is pulling Jono to his feet and dragging him towards the diner. He's barely conscious and keeps muttering to himself about Mina. My arm is taken by Sebastian and, fuck me! I allow him to.

'You are coming with me,' he says. 'I want to know exactly who you are to Mina.'

We're Off to See the Wizard…

Mina's Online Blog 1st August

Bright white light is all I remember and the smell of burning.

I was just about to attack Robratto and whoosh I was gone and in this place. The only way I can describe it is like a large hall filled with varying different people. How the fuck did I get here in the first place? As I move further into the crowd the idea of this place being a hall changes. It's more like a train station. No one is paying any attention to me and I feel totally alone, until my arm is grabbed.

'Jeus…'

'Not that name. Not here,' Uz whispers.

'What?' I ask confused.

'This is the time that you need to watch your mouth,' he says. 'I can't believe Lorreli sent you up here and I allowed it.'

'Where are we?'

Suddenly, the place silences and to my horror every person drops to the floor on their knees leaving me standing. Just before I'm pulled on the floor, I catch sight of a tall woman complete with wings.

'Keep your head down,' Uz hisses. 'I need to work out how to get you out of here.'

'Why? Where the fuc…?'

Uz's hand slams over my mouth.

'Mina, I'm warning you, shut up.'

I give him an apologetic look enough to get him to remove his hand. This must be really serious if he's physically silenced me. He usually just lets me rant while he only half listens. He removes his hand and I mouth an apology.

'Now listen to me very carefully, we are going to slowly back out on our knees and go somewhere out of the way so I can work out to get you out of here. Is that clear?'

I nod at him and wait for him to tell me what to do next, but another voice sounds out in the room.

'Uzrel, why don't you just bring the Marley woman with you to the front.'

It's like the parting of the red sea as every individual turns towards us and opens a path way leading to what I'm assuming is an angel.

I look back at Uz who seems to have grown very pale and nervous.

'What do we do?' I mouth.

'I don't know,' he mouths back.

'Well everyone's looking,' I whisper.

'I know full well everyone's looking Mina, I am not blind.'

'Uzrel, don't keep me waiting,' the angel says.

Slowly getting to our feet, both Uz and I make our way through the crowd to where the angel waits. It feels like the green mile or something and I hate the fact we are being watched like convicts. As we get to angel, Uz drops a knee at her feet leaving me standing. I catch the angel smirk as Uz drags me back to my knees.

'My apologies ma'am, I can explain. I know it's forbidden,' he splutters.

'Come,' she says.

We follow her out of the large room and into what looks like Sebastian's library. A large fire place is lit along one wall with a two leather sofas beside it. Old oil paintings line the walls and the contrast to outside is amazing and a little pretentious.

'So, Uzrel, what is your excuse?' the angel ask.

'It was Lorreli, ma'am, we were protecting Mina, which is what we are supposed to be doing,' Uz answers.

'You brought a demon here of all places,' the angels says.

'Hello,' I wave. 'I'm here. I'm also angel and the incarnation of the first of God's women.'

I see Uz flinch as the angel turns her eyes towards me.

'The key word in that comment is incarnation. Do you know what that word means?' she says.

'Yes, of course…'

'It means to embody the traits of a spirit or the divine in the flesh,' she continues as though I've not spoken. 'The key word again is trait. You are the incarnation of Lilith, but only carry her traits. You are still a half breed that shouldn't be here.'

I open my mouth to counter her, but find I can't, because she's right.

'Do you even know where you are?' she asks.

'Can I guess?' I ask.

'Be my guest,' she smirks.

'Heaven?'

This gets a roaring of laughter from the angel and Uz looks at me with sympathy.

'Mina, this is not heaven. This isn't even close. You wouldn't be able to see any of us there. This is like holding space in-between. Where we angels come and get our orders. The resting place of the angels.'

'Oh,' I say.

Now I feel even more stupid, but in my defence how was I supposed to know.

'Is there any need for rudeness, Ana?'

The angel called Ana suddenly bows her head and in walks the most beautiful man I've ever seen. His skin is like ebony and with no hair on his head, he shines like a beacon. It's his eyes that I recognise. That bright emerald green that are filled with so much knowledge.

'You remind me of Gabriel,' I stutter.

'And how is that brother of mine? Still mooning after the Marley women past and present?'

I shrug because I've nothing to respond with. I'm not entirely comfortable with discussing Gabriel's affections towards me with anyone and it's surprising how defensive I feel about it.

'Forgive me, I am being rude,' the angel offers his hand. 'I am Raphael, may I offer my condolences for the loss of your father, I'm sure Ana here offered hers.'

Ana lowers her head even further, because I suspect Raphael knows damn well she hasn't. I'm liking him already.

'You may leave us,' he tells her.

'But, Master…'

'Ana, please don't make me repeat myself.'

She hurries out of the room leaving just the three us. Raphael sits down and tells us to do the same. I find I'm sat so close to Uz, I may as well as be sitting on his knee, so I try and force some space between us.

'Finally, we are alone. Look, it doesn't take a genius to realise that you shouldn't be here. Thankfully the fact you're half angel is keeping you alive up here. But I don't blame Lorreli or you Uzrel for this. You have both done what you were told. However to bring her here is just has dangerous. Do you know who leads the Emandato?'

Uzrel shakes his head. 'No Master.'

'Then it seems you are the last to know and you are her guardian,' Raphael sighs.

'I don't know,' I offer.

Raphael laughs. 'You are such a sweetheart for a succubus. The person or angel who is leading the Emandato is my brother and I'm sure I don't need to say his name.'

Uz's body tenses beside me, while I try and work out my angel lore to who he means. Then it hits me as I start to open my mouth Uz clasps a hand over it.

'Don't say his name. Not here,' he says.

'Why is it like say the J' name?' I ask.

'It's worse.'

'I think what Uzrel is trying to say is that we angels are good at picking up vibrations and while the presence of your angel godparents have kept you safe in Supton, the same cannot be said here. Here you are on his turf and by saying his name it will bring him straight to you.'

'He's the one that…you know…with you know. He's not one to mess with,' I ask.

Fear is now chilling my body. Out of all the archangels to hate me it had to be that one. Now Uz is pulling me to my feet. His body is actually shaking with his own fear.

'I need to get her out of here now,' he says.

'Not yet, you can't. The Power wants to speak to her,' Raphael says.

'Why do they want to do that?' Uz asks.

'Uzrel, my brother, I said The Power.'

'But that can't…Mina is not a full angel it will kill her.'

Now I'm starting to really panic about who wants to speak to me.

'You need to tell me who you're talking about,' I ask. 'Because I'm thinking all sorts of crap.'

Raphael smile broadens as he gets to his feet. He towers over us, not just in height, but in broadness too.

'Uzrel, don't panic we will use the Curtain,' Raphael says.

'What the hell is the Curtain?' I ask, the word spilling out before I can stop it and to my surprise Raphael roars with laughter as Uz, clearly embarrassed tries to smile.

'The Curtain is a way for you to safely commune with the Power. Think of yourself as Dorothy in Oz.'

'You've seen that movie?' I ask.

He puts his arm around my shoulder as he walks me and Uz from the room.

'I'm a sucker for the films humans make,' he says. 'It's a weakness.'

We walk through the rest of the angels who all bow as we pass, before going about their business. I imagine Micka here amongst all his family.

'The Militants do not come here,' Raphael says.

'I wasn't…' I splutter.

'No of course you wasn't,' he smirks. 'The Militants go straight up. They don't belong here.'

We continue to walk until amongst the angels and I realise that there's barely any sound. No-one is talking to each other. It should feel uneasy, but I just feel peaceful.

'They come here to cleanse themselves of the human world. Angels are sensitive to everything and here they can align themselves once more,' Raphael offers.

That does seem to make sense, almost like a spa for angels and to be fair being human can be a little toxic. Finally, we come to another doorway and Raphael opens the door for Uz and I step through. He leads through a long corridor that is lined with doors and I start to feel a little closed in. If possible the place feels smaller. Thankfully, Raphael stops outside one of the doors and gives me a smile.

'I will leave you here. Both of you and once He has finished, you will be sent back home. All I'll say Mina is don't be tempted to look beyond the curtain. The room has only just been cleaned after the last occurrence.' Shock must be on my face, because he starts to laugh. 'Don't fret child. You will be fine. Now I must say my goodbyes and if you see any of my brothers down there, tell them to get their head out of their arses.'

Then he's gone leaving Uz and I alone. We look at each other for a moment before speaking.

'Have you done this before?' I ask.

'Not using the Curtain,' he answers. 'Let's just get this done. The quicker we do the quicker you'll be back in Supton.'

Opening the door, we both step into the most boring room in the world. I don't know what I expected. Hissing machines everywhere, but all there is two chairs in the middle of a square room. There's not even a curtain for fucks sake. We take a seat and as we do Uz shakes his head slightly. It's as though he knows what I'm thinking and telling me to shut up.

Then I feel it. My body responding to everything in the room. It's as though I am connected to everything and I can feel it. The sensitivity in my body is increased and suddenly, everything I'm wearing and even the chair, I'm sitting is becoming uncomfortable to the point of painful.

'Uz, I can't breathe,' I manage and he takes my hand.

'Yes you can just breathe normally, you are panicking.'

I try and do the old breathing through my nose and out through my mouth, but it's not working. In fact, I'm sure I'm going to faint. Please make it stop, I think. Whatever is pulling at me is making me hurt and I don't like it. Then it stops and there in front of me, I'm sure there's a shimmer like a curtain. The air settles and I feel able to breathe once more.

'Should we kneel?' I whisper to Uz.

'That is not necessary Mina Marley,' a voice booms.

I nearly jump from my seat to my knees just in reaction, but I manage to keep my arse where it is.

'So, Lorreli sent you up here, knowing full well it is forbidden. No human has ever set foot in this place. Yet here you are.'

'Yes sir,' I manage.

I'm not sure how to address the voice and Uz isn't really helping me either.

'Well I've been keeping an eye on everything in Supton and there are a few things not pleasing me. For one Uzrel, you are supposed to be her guardian, yet you allowed your own issues cloud your judgement. You hid up here. Why did you leave your post?'

Turning towards Uz, I see he's playing nervous with his fingers. It's like seeing a little boy get told off by the headmaster and I suddenly feel all defensive.

'The guy was trying to do his best,' I argue.

'I'm sorry. I should have tried harder. I should have not let her seduce me,' Uz says.

'And why did that happen?' the voice says.

'Er hello! I thought you wanted to talk to me,' I say.

'It happened because…' Uz stutters.

I'm being ignored and normally that would piss me off, but I'm also interested to know why he let that happen.

'Because…?' the voice asks.

'Because I was jealous and I wanted her to love me like she does Micka.'

'What?!'

He's got my full attention now. What the…where the fuck has that come from? Uz now seems to looking on the verge of panic.

'You've got to understand I've been there from the very beginning. Even closer than Williamina when she was guardian, so to know she loves him more than me stings. So when she tried to seduce me, it felt good.'

'Seriously?' I ask and he shrugs. 'You got jealous? You have feelings like that for me?'

'I cannot deny it. Not here,' he whispers.

I'm beyond exasperated.

'What is wrong with you people? Do I wear some sort of perfume,' I say.

Uz hangs his head and it pulls at my heart strings too much.

'Tell him, Mina,' the voice says.

My heart jumps. That person can't know that. It was long ago. So long ago.

'Tell me what?'

'Okay!' I say. 'Okay,' I repeat taking a deep breath. 'I did have a sorta crush on you.'

Uz's head snaps up. 'When?'

Now it's my turn to feel uncomfortable. 'I was twelve or thirteen.'

'Oh whoopdie doo. I was part of a school girl crush.'

'Well I'm sooo sorry. Would it make you feel better if you know that I cried for a whole week, because I knew you wouldn't love me?'

'All I'm saying is it would be nice to be appreciated,' he argues, before the voice booms: silence at us.

Both of us sit quietly and barely mutter apologies.

'Now, I wanted to talk to you Mina about being on this crash course you seem to putting yourself through. You've been given the very person that completes you and yet you seem determined on making his life a misery.'

'I don't mean to. I never asked for all of this,' I say.

'Then learn some gratitude. Go back and end this fiasco once and for all.'

I bristle at the word gratitude. The word that has haunted my life since childhood. Uz senses this and takes me hand and squeezes it.

'I have the gift of free will and it's a right I will exercise,' I manage to say calmly.

'You of course are right and if that's your choice then maybe we should exercise our right to pull out any intervention we have given you.'

'You won't do that. You need me,' I bluff.

'You are a mere speck of dust to us and your ego will be the ruin of you,' the voice answers.

Something doesn't feel right here. This voice is supposed to be the Power. That's what Raphael said and I'm assuming that this power is God, but this doesn't sound like a conversation with God. There's someone else behind this curtain. Another wizard playing a part and the realisation of the fact is making me dizzy. We are being played. God would never speak to either of us like that. Getting out of the chair, Uz grabs at my hand.

'What are you doing?' he hisses.

'Do you trust me?'

'No,' he answers bluntly.

Ignoring him, I make my way across the room to where the shimmering curtain hangs.

'Mina Marley, sit down,' the voice booms.

Uz grabs at my arm and tries to drag me away, but I pull away. I want to know what's behind the curtain.

'Uzrel, control your charge,' the voice demands.

This time I'm grabbed fully by Uz, but I fight against him as I reach the curtain. With a swift kick at Uz, that I have no time to feel guilty about, I get free and jump through the curtain. Only to be hit by the Curtain's power field that I expect to throw me across the room, but another hand grabs me and drags me into a beautiful white room.

'You are Lilith inside and out,' the owner of the hand says.

Once my eyes adjust to the brightness, I see the voice we've been speaking to. A short old man looks at me with a disapproving glare. He actually reminds me of my father and my heart twinges. What follows, is the realisation of who he could be.

'God!'

The word comes out before I can stop it and now he smiles.

'Really, you think He would come here and talk to you. My earlier assertion of your ego still stands.'

'So who are you?' I ask.

'I have many names,' he answers cryptically.

'How about just one,' I throw.

'I am the one that made Lilith. It was my hands that moulded both you and Adam. I was given the plans and I followed them. I am your creator and my name is Joe. The voice, the eyes and hands of the highest power in the world.'

'Joe? Your name is *Joe*?' I ask a little astonished at such a simple name for someone so important.

He looks at me like I'm the stupidest thing he's ever met.

'Joe is what I prefer,' he says. 'I'm going to send you back with your guardian, but know this, you have free will. All of God's people have that. You choose your path, but there will be a sacrifice. If you do not accept Sebastian and marry him, then I will take the one who really holds your heart and tear him to pieces right in front of you.'

My throat constricts. I can't believe this little old man has just said that to me.

'Why would you do that?' I choke.

'Because, Mina, you have to learn that I created you and what I want and say goes. I'm sick to death of watching you take liberties. Now go, you are no longer welcome in my presence.'

And I'm back in my flat, with Uz beside me. His face is flushed and he's breathless.

'What on earth…what possessed you to…? How did you manage to not die?'

'I'm sorry, Uz, but I had to find out who we were speaking to.'

'And did you find out who it was?' he asks.

'Yeah, some angel called Joe. He said he was my creator.'

Uz looks like I've just punched him hard in the chest and now I'm seriously regretting my actions.

'You met Joe?' he whispers.

'Yes, he said he's the creator.'

'And what did he say?'

'I think you know what he said to me. It seems I'm to buy a wedding dress.'

Uz reaches out and pulls me into a hug.

'I wish with all my heart I had the power to let you choose freely. Know I've fought them every step of the way, but I can't risk you going against them.'

I nod into his chest. I know this. Uz has only ever wanted the best for me, but he's just as powerless as I am. No matter what, Micka and I have to be over. It's time to cut my ties with him once and for all. There can be nothing left holding us together.

'Uz, how do I release Micka from his vow?'

Uz looks down at me.

'Is that wise?' he asks.

'It's the only way. Micka and I are over.'

Candice and Lorreli

Candice's Journal 1st August 0945hrs

The nightmares are getting worse and nothing Lorreli does can erase the sight of Robratto's body from my mind. My hands killed him, not matter who the fuck was controlling me. I don't understand why I had to do it and not Mina. Is the angelicdemon more precious than me? Well fuck that. I am a person too.

'Mina needs you to be strong,' she says.

'But what about me?' I argue. 'Why is it all about Mina?'

'It's not about Mina. It's about you and her together.'

And that's all I get from her. I'm so fucking exhausted I can't think straight.

Morag offered for me to return to Faeterrea with her, but Lorreli advised me to sit and ride it out. In the end Morag left, but not without telling me that no angel should rule a Fae.

You know I wish the two sides would get along. These past few months surely have taught us to get a grip and move on. I'm getting seriously fucked off with all this political crap that comes out of their mouths. In the end, I ignore even Lorreli and crawl back to bed. I need to hide for a little bit. Recover from all the stress they are putting me under. If they want me strong then they have to leave me alone to deal with it first.

Then this morning waking up, I felt a little stronger and better. Lorreli had left me alone and my sleep was not disturbed. Whether she helped with that I've no idea. However that was soon to change.

I had flash of lightening moment while in the shower. A moment of: *oh my fucking god.* Stumbling from the bathroom, I find the book that Nanna had left me and read through the origin of all Others. The birth of Lilith, and how she helped save us from annulation from the angels. The one bit, I seemed to skip through boredom.

When Lilith left the garden, the angels sent the Militant leader, Micka to find and kill her. The Powers didn't want God's first woman roaming free beyond the garden. Lilith was already making changes and the Others were listening to her.

The Others were scattering and some were developing powers as Lilith was sharing her god given powers. However, Lilith had an angel on her shoulder and Gabriel was keen to keep her hidden and protected. He loved her more than any of his brothers and sister, but his father would not punish him.

But the angels had other problems. They were starting to separate into two camps. Those that wanted the Others dead and those who felt that they should live with God's people. The leaders of these two camps were Lucifer and Michael. Lucifer argued that the new God's race should not be favoured and took the argument to his father. Michael responded in anger and decided the only way to end this once and for all was to cut off the snake's head. Lilith had to die.

Using Micka, the strongest of all Militants, once more they both scoured the land for her, but she remained hidden, until one summer night she was found. God's first human daughter asleep with her twin children. Micka under Michael's instruction took the girl child from her mother and held her hostage, Lilith woke to the sound of her daughter cries and tried to attack the Militant, but he was too strong and the child was destroyed in front of her.

The scream from Lilith shook the ground as the sky opened up and rained hail and water.

'You will pay,' she screamed at the Militant.

'It is you that will pay,' the Militant swore. 'Now, it is you and your bastard son's turn. You are an abomination to your father.'

'Please allow my son to run free,' she pleaded.

The Militant refused. His orders clear. Lilith should die. Knowing there was nothing she could do, she took her son in her arms and kneeled at the Militant's feet.

'Make it quick,' she said.

Just as the Militant prepared to end Lilith's life, there was a crash of thunder and the brightest of lights.

'Stop!' A voice boomed. 'I command you Militant by the powers of the Great Power to leave this woman alone.'

The Militant bowed and took a step back, before disappearing. Lilith looked up with a tear stained face and saw the most beautiful angel with majestic white wings. Her long dark hair shone like ebony and she stood tall and proud. The breast plate shone brightly, reflecting the moonlight.

'Rise child,' she said.

Lilith struggled to her feet with her son still in her arms.

'Who are you?'

'I am Canaan. The blood sister of Gabriel, Michael and Lucifer. The first of the four and the revered daughter of the Great Father.'

'Why are you saving me?' Lilith asked.

'Because Michael is wrong. The Great Father wanted you to live for a reason. The Powers, however are not your friend. I follow only the orders from HIM, not Them.'

'They've killed my daughter,' Lilith cried.

'And because he has, Michael has placed a curse on her. Sons will only be born free. Any daughter will be condemned and cursed. I cannot lift it, but I can change it. Your bloodline will continue strong, but I will only allow a few daughters to be born.'

'So you are allowing me my freedom?' Lilith asked.

'I'm allowing your freedom, but I know my time is short and I things are changing for us. We are on the cusp of war. You must stay safe and, Gabriel nor I will be able to protect you much longer. However, I will give you a gift.'

Asking Lilith to hold out her hand, Cannan offered her ball of white light that disappeared into Lilith's body. At first Lilith squirmed and fell to the floor in pain, before a pair of dark wings emerged on her back.

'What have you done?' Lilith asked breathlessly.

'I have given you part of my angelic essence. This will keep you safe until I return. We are joined as one now and no-one will harm you.'

'What if you never return?'

Canaan smiled. 'I will return Lilith. It may not be in this lifetime, but I will return and when I do, we both will stand strong together and unite the two worlds as one.'

And Canaan did leave and did not return. The war raged and Lucifer was sent to the underworld. Canaan was banished too and became the mother of the Faes. Her first born would become the first of all Faes.

But her promise remained. She would return and with Lilith they would unite the two worlds of the Others and God's people as one.

The book shakes in my hands as I try and take it all in and what Gabriel has said to Morag. Lorreli is silent, but I can feel her tension. She's close. Very close to me. Waiting for me.

'Your name is not Lorreli is it?' I say slowly.

'No,' she whispers.

'And the reason you have no body…?'

'Is because I had to wait for it to be born and ready for its real soul to enter it.'

'What do you mean real soul? What have I got now?'

Lorreli takes a moment to answer until I yell at her.

'What sort of soul have I got now?'

'You have the soul that you were meant to have, but it's just missing a small piece. I am that missing piece.'

'Which means?'

'You and I are the same. I have no body, because that body is you. I just had to wait for you to be ready to accept me.'

'I thought you were an angel?' I whisper.

'Go to the mirror,' she says.

I go into the bathroom at her request and look at my reflection then there's a wave in the air and I see a shadow of myself standing behind me. It's faint, but I can still see. There is something else. Something that I've always craved, but never had. A pair of beautiful white wings shadowed behind me.

'This is me,' Lorreli says. 'What I really look like…'

'Like me, because you are me,' I whisper. 'What is your name?'

'I think you already know,' she says.

I lurch towards the toilet and throw up what breakfast I'd managed to eat. I don't want to hear any of this. It's too fucking big to handle.

'Say our name,' Lorreli says.

'No, fuck off,' I choke.

'Sweetheart, if you are to feel complete then you must say our name,' she pushes.

'My…our name is Canaan.'

'You've returned. Now we go back to Faeterrea and tell them.'

Walking the Line

Tannini's Journal 4th August 2245hrs

The clean-up of Robratto was trickier than I ever expected. Hearing from Gabriel that the leader was Michael and knowing he could arrive at any moment, scared me shitless. Give him his dues, Gabriel helped me and my men and soon it was as though nothing had happened. The Robrattos line gone. Finished. Or we have to assume.

But knowing it's Michael that's after Mina fucks with my head. He's a purist. Us Others are the enemy. I know that much from the history. He not only defeated Lucifer, he tried to abolish us too. Not that I advocate Lucifer either. That son of a bitch had his own motives and issues. That's why you never hear or see anything of him. Even the fucking demons are clueless.

I asked Gabriel what we should do and he merely said he'd deal with it. This town is protected.

'What about Mina?'

'Lorreli would have sent her somewhere safe and with Uzrel. Once they return, we as a town need to stand behind her. Do you think all the Elders will accept her as their queen and protect her?' he asks.

'I can't speak for the other Elders, but the Council will stand by her. But assuming they've spent the time to come here. I don't see any issues.'

Beverly was waiting for me when I returned. Her pale face, rigid with fear. Of course I went to embrace her, but was pushed away.

'Tell me it's not true,' she said to me.

It takes a moment for me to try and understand what she's talking about and I'm still a little fucked off that she's just pushed me away.

'I would have told you if I'd have known, but I didn't. She just turned up on my fucking door step and bang I'm a dad,' I answer.

Beverley looked at me confused for a moment.

'I already knew about Samantha,' she said. 'This is about Michael being the leader of the Emandato.'

'What?' I said. 'You knew about Sammy? When were you going to tell me?'

She looked at me flustered. Her face now flushed. I'd caught her out and it stung.

'Look, I'm not here about whether you knocked up some woman years ago. I want to know about Michael. You do know he has the power to destroy all of us,' she snapped.

'I am aware Beverley, but I've not told you, because I've only fucking found out and you seem keen on giving me the cold shoulder.'

I may as well have slapped her, because she took a step back before slumping onto my sofa.

'I love you Stan,' she said. 'But right now, I can't think about that. Michael will destroy us and the thought of never seeing you again rips me in two. I'm trying to save myself from a broken heart.'

How could I argue with that? I couldn't I even stay mad at her when she's crying. Bloody women.

Now, she's just left me again after we made love once more. I tried to reassure her about Michael, but she wouldn't hear it. I can't blame her, but I also believe that having Gabriel onside will work for us.

Mina Online Blog 4th August 2330hrs.

The days after coming back from the angel train station as I'm now calling it. Left me a little worse for wear. I'm constantly exhausted and throwing my guts up at anything and everything. Uz assures me that this is normal, but doesn't hide the worry on his face. I know I shouldn't have been there and can't help wondering if they are just making me suffer for it.

The first thing I did on my return was drive to the Manor. I needed to make amends with Sebastian. Yet again. After he asked me if I was alright, he was shocked at Lorreli's actions, but not surprised and where I thought there'd be a fight, there wasn't. Neither did he ask me questions about what I'd seen or heard. Leaving me to wonder if he's scared of what they all think of him too. But for now, he's just understanding and when I say I want to confirm a date, he agrees.

'We need to do this in a month,' I say.

'I couldn't agree more. We'll do it on September the First,' he answers. 'I'll arrange someone to perform the union.'

Normally weddings in Supton are done with the Others priest or priestess. But for me and Sebastian, we are a little different. I assume Uz may do it, but Sebastian doesn't think he has the power.

'Gabriel could do it,' I say.

Sebastian physically flinches at the suggestion and it takes me a moment to realise why.

'I'm sorry,' I fluster. 'He just is an archangel.'

'I know and you're right, and he does want us to be together. It's time to end this silly feud with him. I will ask him,' Sebastian says.

I then tell him, what I've asked Uz to help me do. I'm sure there are tears in his eyes.

'Are you sure that is what you want?' he asks.

'It's the only way.'

'Then it must be your choice. I will not stand in your way. He's yours to do as you will.'

So, I go back the flat–the source of my power according to legend. I've no idea what it will entail. All I want is not to hurt him. I don't want that. I just need to be free of him and he of me. Don't get me wrong, I love with him all my heart, but if Joe can destroy him then the thought of that is too much for me to bear. Uz meets me and I ask him if Micka needs to be here and he shakes his head.

'Does he know?' I ask.

'He will know when the act is done.'

'Will he feel anything?'

'If it had been just godparent and child, then hardly anything, but the bond you've both created is so strong that he will feel that break in his heart.'

This doesn't sit well at all, but I've no other choice. I've got to rip this damn plaster off.

'What do I need to do?'

Uz instructs me in what is needed. My expulsion rite last time had rid me of the tattoo, which was my biggest connection. What this will do, I've no idea.

'We will cut every bond you've created with him, emotionally and sexually. You both will be free of the other. He will go back to being owned by the Powers.'

'Then let's get it over with,' I say.

Sitting on a dining room chair, in the middle of my living room, I nervously wait while Uz prepares the space around me. Purifying it so nothing can hit back at me or him. His slow muttering is making me edgy. I know I'm doing the right thing, but this is really goodbye. No false starts or forgetting each other. This is me saying I've made my choice.

'Are you ready?' Uz asks finally.

'Yes.'

'And you are sure? Once we free him, he will return back to the Powers and will never be used to protect you ever again.'

Taking a deep breath I nod.

'Say it Mina. Tell me you are sure,' Uz commands.

'Yes I am sure.'

'Then we will begin.'

He hands me a piece of paper and I look down at it questionably.

'What is this?'

'The vows we took when you were born. These are Micka's.'

I scan the paper quickly. He swore to protect me for the rest of my life. To lay his own life down for me and love me unconditionally. The last bit punches me hard in the chest. I bet he never expected to love me like he does.

'Mina, are you ready?' Uz asks.

'What do I need to do?'

'Simple, these are his vows. Tell him that you release him from every vow he made. While you do, I'll cut each tie. It may hurt, but continue to repeat those words until I tell you to stop. Is that clear?'

'Yes,' I whisper.

'Then begin.'

'Micka, my guide, my protector, I release you from protecting me…'

The pain that ripples through my body is intense and it takes my breath away. Down on my knees pain, Uz continues to chant his own stuff too. He told me it would hurt, but I wasn't prepared for how much. I have to continue.

'Micka, my guide, my protector, I release you from laying down your life for me…oh god,' I scream.

Uz doesn't stop. His flow can't be broken even if his eyes are full of sympathy. His hands moving in slicing motions around and above me. No doubt cutting through all invisible ties. I don't know why I expected it to be like when I first met Sebastian and my father wanted me to release my godparents then. But that was fake. I never let any of them go. It was show. This is real. This feels like every part of me is being ripped to pieces.

My body is soaked in sweat as I rock on my knees to try and ease the pain. Sitting on the chair has long gone. The last part, I know is going to be agonizing. It's about strength. For the sake of the man I love then I must be strong, and just as I prepare for the last part, there he appears in front for me. On his knees, his face is ghost white as he seems to fade in and out of my room like mirage. I don't understand what's happening and Uz seems unfazed. Like he knew this would happen. He'd promised he would feel no pain.

'Mina, what are you doing?' he pleads.

I look up at Uz who is still chanting, but he gives me the slightest nod of his head. Keep going. Just keep going.

'Micka, my guide, my protector, I release you for loving me. Your heart and my heart will no longer be bound…Uz, I can't…'

Micka and I are both screaming now in pain and this time Uz stops. The urge to reach out and hold Micka is strong. Make it better and stop the pain, and right there and then, I'm torn between head and heart.

'Shall I continue?' Uz asks.

'Please don't release me,' Micka pleads.

I'm in agony not just physically, but seeing what I'm doing to Micka is too much. Uz never told me that this would happen. I thought I'd be here on my own.

'Mina, I will leave here, but don't release me. I beg you. Everything will disappear. Our memories. Our love. Don't take that way.'

Uz grabs my face in his hands so I focus on him.

'This isn't really Micka. It's the illusion your heart and mind has created. Do you want me to carry on?'

'Yes,' I manage.

Uz places a hand on my heart and it's as though my heart is reaching for his grasp. He mutters some words and I wait with baited breathe for my heart to be ripped out, but nothing happens. Uz looks at me and a frown creases his brow.

'Uz please, I need to the pain to stop. Just do it.'

He mutters again, but still nothing and then with a flash of white light, Gabriel appears and throws Uz across my room.

'You stupid arsehole,' he screams.

Uz scrambles to his knees and presses his head to the floor. But Gabriel is not letting him off that easy. Pulling him to his feet, Gabriel punches Uz over and over again until blood pours from his face. With barely any strength left, all my protectiveness takes over and ripples to the surface and with all mighty scream to stop, I floor Gabriel with my own inner power.

'You fool,' Gabriel gasps.

'I asked him to do it,' I shout. 'You want me to have Sebastian then this is the deal. I lose Micka.'

'Uzrel, do you realise what you were allowing her to do and the consequences of those actions?' Gabriel says.

'Master, I just wanted her to be free,' Uz grovels.

Gabriel's own shuddering breath stalls for a minute, before he speaks.

'I knew it was a bad idea using angels as your godparents. You Mina are the only incarnation that seems capable of bringing us to our knees.'

'I'm trying to make life easier between Sebastian and I,' I say.

'Then doing this isn't the answer. Don't you understand, Micka is the strongest and most powerful of all Militants. Even now, in his love sick state, he's still the best we have. If you release him from his vow then he returns to his former state.'

'Yes I already know this,' I push.

There's a gasp in the corner where Uz still is crouched.

'I'm sorry Master,' he repeats.

Obviously, I'm wearing a confused look on my face, because Gabriel growls at me in frustration.

'Mina, think about it. If Micka returns to his former state then he can be used by Michael to kill you. The only reason you are safe is because that weapon is not only your property, but is madly in love with you.'

Jesus fucking Christ that never even entered my head. To even think that Micka is my biggest threat and a weapon to use against me, fucks me over. Why did I ever allow us to be intimate? The simple answer is because I love him just as much.

'Why didn't you tell me?' I ask Uz.

'I swear I didn't know,' he says.

'It's okay, you can't know everything,' I reassure him.

My body is starting to calm down now and the pain has ceased. The three of us sit down and take a moments breather. I make Gabriel apologise to Uz and he gives it reluctantly, but he does give it.

'Is Micka okay?' I ask. 'I didn't hurt him.'

Gabriel gives me the smallest of smiles.

'He has no idea. The mirage was me sending you a warning. Trying to appeal to your heart, but you are so stubborn.'

'I know,' I smile back.

'Uzrel, will you leave us.'

Uz looks at me and I give him a nod and a big hug.

'I'm sorry I got you in trouble,' I offer.

'I would do it again.'

Then he's gone leaving me alone with Gabriel.

'How are you feeling?'

'I'm not in pain anymore,' I say.

'I meant after you going to the Station?'

'Is that what it's really called? I thought it was a joke,' I laugh.

'No, we do have a name for it, but here, you would not know the words.'

'You're brother Raphael passed on a message. He said you need to get your head out of your arse,' I say.

He laughs again, but it's got a hint of sadness to it.

'He is the peacekeeper. Always has been. But you didn't answer my question, how are you feeling?'

'I'm okay, it's just the sickness. I'm throwing up all the time.'

'I'm sure that will pass,' he says. 'The journey can be an ordeal for any. I hear you've set a date and you requested that I be the one to marry you.'

'It seemed fitting,' I answer. 'Will you do it?'

Gabriel turns his body towards me and it's hard not to see the sadness there.

'I will, but only because you asked me. Now go home to Sebastian and prepare for your wedding.'

Later that night, Sebastian doesn't ask about if I released Micka or not. Maybe he knows. He seems to know everything, but I appreciate him not asking me. The show of trust must be growing between us.

The Woman in Black

Ray's Journal written by Danny Marley 10th August 1135hrs

I've been moved in for over a week into my old family home. It's strange being back in these four walls. My sister and I were born here, I know every inch of this place, yet it doesn't feel like home any more.

Ray's stuff is still here and that's when I found this and his other journals. It's taken so long to read through as well as emotionally draining. It's not good to go over the past, especially when that past is painful.

Now, I'm writing in it. It feels like sacrilege, but I'm compelled anyway. I'm no writer. Food is my passion. It's where Jonathan gets it from. I worked in old Dave's in the good old days and would often be called upon to bake cakes for the town. Birthdays, weddings anything. What I could do with icing and sugar craft was the stuff of legend. It's how I met Magda. I baked her sweet sixteen birthday cake.

That was before the change. Deanna and I were not like Jonathan and Mina. We knew what we were. Our heritage. Our parents were both from hell. Our father, a Marley pure and mother another sucubbus. Their sole purpose was to bring us into the world. There was no love or romance. They fucked and created a pair pure born twins and that was that. Our mother disappeared soon after we were born and our father hired a nanny to take care of us until he died fourteen years later.

Our home life wasn't exactly warm and loving, our father barely wanted anything to do with me. His interest was Deanna. She was a Marley female. That made her special. There was no angel involvement then. He never allowed it.

'They are as corrupt as any demon,' he would say.

But once he died all that protection went and in they swooped and the Marleys control over Supton ended.

Deanna and I managed to live as normal as we could. Going to school, thinking of careers. All normal stuff. Magda and I were dating and then angels came more often as Deanna reached seventeen and that's when it all went wrong.

This house is full of so little happiness for me. It's a damn curse. No wonder Mina wouldn't live here.

Now I hear that Michael is back and wanting to finish what he started. The only blessing we have against that psycho is that Mina owns the bigger weapon. There is also more news. Gabriel tells me that there are signs of another generation of Marley.

'Mina is pregnant?' I asked.

'I thought so, but no,' he replies. 'I felt something when she killed Laura, but then it's gone.'

'Which leaves Jonathan,' I finish.

He has yet to say anything to me, but there's the possibility that he doesn't know. He swore to me that he would be careful, but if some poor girl out there is unwittingly carry a Marley line then she better hope that child doesn't survive. Cruel as it sounds. The future of a Marley is hard one, girl or boy. That is a given.

Email from Jaq to Carla 9th August 2300hrs

Hello Hun,

I know it's really late, but I just wanted you to know I got back home safe. Thank you so much for all your advice and comfort. I've already made the appointment and feel a little better about my choice. Like you said. Hold strong for a little longer and it will be done.

Love you loads and will message you when done.

Jaq

Mina's Online Blog 11th August 2330hrs.

My life was already upside down, but I was just about accepting things when someone just grabbed the rug and pulled it right from beneath me. How many more lies is there that I need to find out about?

The day had started off kinda okay. Jaq and I were in Angela's Bridal Shop, going through dresses. Trying to find something suitable was hardwork, both Jaq and I have differing views on dress. She's all puffball and fuss and I'm…well you all know me. I found out the difference between princess and empire lines, and sweetheart necklines. Boned or unboned bodice. Who the fuck cares?

With my size and figure, I'm thinking of just a simple white dress with no frills. A classic cut. This wedding is more about show than fairytale endings. Angela is all excited. She'll have been told that money is no issue by Sebastian. Money signs are in her eyes and the snotty bitch is being nice as pie.

Angela is a Fae and up her own arse and I've had little do with her. She tried to attach herself to my father when I was younger. She had her eye on the house. The first golddigger, before Lydia.

Finally, after what seemed like torturous hours, I picked something suitable and to appease, both myself and Jaq. I'd yet to mention that I wanted both she and Candice as my bridesmaids. I thought I'd just drop that in casually another time.

Mina's was open as usual and Jaq and I took our afternoon shifts there. It was nice to be in my normal environment. My customers were starting to come back to me. I think they need the normality. Good food and drink always brings people back together.

I appreciate that people are not talking to me about recent events. Just regular gossip as though nothing has happened. It's peaceful. Just like the days before the Cycle. No-one's even mentioned the Lilith thing. I wonder how many actually know the story. How many were told to keep it a secret.

It must have been the dinner time shift when I first saw her. Standing across the street looking towards the diner. Still wearing black, but this time looking more like a fifties screen idol with headscarf and glasses. I tried to ignore her, but you know what it's like when you know you're being watched, you get creeped out. Twenty minutes she stayed there, before I'd had enough. Walking out of Mina's, I shouted towards her and fuck me, she disappeared into thin air.

Running inside, I rang Tannini and he came straight over where I closed us into my office.

'Do you think it's something do with Michael and the Emandato?' I asked.

'Who knows. You should talk to Gabriel and I'll add more security around Mina's' he offers. 'Maybe Micka can help.'

I hadn't spoken to him since we sat on his bed, but Tannini is right. Micka is the only weapon I can use, but I can't think straight about him right now. But getting that woman out of my head was proving difficult. Then an idea hit me like a hammer and I shouted Gabriel.

'You cannot just summon me at will,' he chastised. 'I am busy with other things.'

I tell him about the woman in black being at the funeral and then standing outside the diner. Then give him my theory, which causes him to try and hide a smirk.

'You think that Eve as in Sebastian's second wife is here in Supton watching his first wife?'

'Yes, why is that funny?' I demand.

'I'm sorry,' Gabriel apologised. 'Look, Mina, Eve had a prolonged life and gave Adam many children, but she died peacefully with her family around her. That woman is not Eve. She'll be one of Michael's whores. Micka is watching over you take comfort in that.'

That's news to me. I thought he'd abandoned me. That feeling of connection must be waning. This should be a good thing, but I'm filled with sadness. Things are changing and moving so fast, I can barely breathe.

'I will try and find out who she is?' he offered.

Then he was gone and I was alone once more. That would be the end of it. I'd forget it. Whoever that bitch was, she wouldn't ruin my day.

Oh how fucking wrong I was.

Everything was ticking over nicely when all of a sudden the ground beneath us began to shake so violently, I was convinced the windows would shatter. Everyone looked at me and all I could offer was a shrug. Bad thing to do, because panic set in and everyone started screaming as rain and hail followed by lightening started to fall.

'What the fuck?' Jaq asked as she and the others hurried out. 'Is it Candice?'

'You know what I haven't seen her in ages,' I said. 'This doesn't feel like her. It feels...different... familiar.'

She gives me a strange look. 'What does that mean?'

I don't get to answer as a bolt of lightning hits the road just in front of us. Then there's silence and uneasiness in the air. We are all waiting for the next strike. My own body tingles with its own power. Charging and ready for action.

'Jaq, how's your faerie magick if we need it?'

'You know it's rusty, but I will give it a go.'

Suddenly from nowhere a car came to a screeching halt and Sebastian and Danny nearly fell out of the car.

'Are you alright?' the both ask.

'Yes, is it the Emandato?'

Looking past them, there she is. The woman in black walking towards us. The smirk she wears frightens me and the power I'm feeling is peaking in my hands ready to throw.

'In the name that is all holy that can't be,' Danny hisses.

He's so unsteady that it's Dom that catches him before he hits the floor.

'Danny, who is it?' I whisper.

'It's impossible,' he mutters.

'Fuck this,' I shout. 'Bitch who the fuck do you think you are coming into my town?'

Just as I am taking a step towards her, not only does Sebastain grab my arm, but every godparent, bar Lorreli appears in front of me. The woman wears a smile.

'Ah the godparents. Missing a few it seems, Mina,' the woman sneers.

'You are not welcome here?' Sebastian says.

'Sebastian dear, I'm Supton's real queen and it's time I took back the crown from my unsurper.'

'You've never been queen,' Sebastian hisses.

Okay so everyone seems to know who this is apart from me and now I'm pissed off.

'Only a Marley can rule here, so like I said bitch, fuck off,' I shout.

The ball of white light leaves me hand before I've even thought about what I've done, but it just seems to bounce off her.

And everyone's voice shouting no at me resounds in my head.

'Aw shucks it seems you're not the only Marley with an angel on their shoulder,' she smiles.

'What?!' I gasp.

'Danny has prison softened you? Come and embrace your sister.'

Breathing is becoming impossible as I see the truth in Danny's eyes.

'You're a liar,' I scream.

In slow motion she pulls free the headscarf and long blood red hair falls over her shoulders. With her glasses removed I see it instantly.

'You're dead,' I whisper.

'We banished you from ever coming back here,' Uz says.

With an almighty scream another bolt strikes and this time it's me.

'Will someone tell me what the fuck is going on and why dead mother is standing in front of me?'

It's Sebastian that comes to my side and wraps his arms around me.

'This isn't the place,' he shouts. 'Deanna we will take this to the Manor. Angels will come too. Right now Mina stays with me.'

'We do it now,' she shouts back.

'Deanna, we go to the Manor.'

I'm hysterical in the car, so far beyond myself, I'm sure I've met myself on the way back. There's not much more I can deal with.

'You told me she was dead,' I rave while punching out at Sebastian and Danny. 'Why do you all fucking lie to me? She was dead.'

'We lied to protect you,' Sebastian says.

'What from? My mother? Are you high?' I scream.

'I told Ray this would all fucking blow up in our faces,' Danny yells at Sebastian.

'You were the one who told us she had killed herself,' Sebastian shouts back.

'And that's what I got told,' Danny hisses.

I'm the first out of the car when it stops and leave Sebastian and Danny in my wake as I run into the Manor. There they all are. Uz, Cladiel and Micka. The three bar my way to my mother, who sits perched on one of the chairs.

This is the true Marley woman. There's no wonder she was admired so much. Her figure is slender, yet strong, with just enough curves to matter. Her eyes are like Jono's and Danny's, the brightest green. I can feel them scrutinising me, but I don't have to wait long for her opinion.

'Seems someone took a little too much after their father,' she says. 'Although, it seems you've got the men in this town wrapped round your little finger, so must have something.'

'What?...why?' I whisper before bursting into tears, the last reaction on earth, yet it's all I can do.

This mother that I'd idolised most of my life is not only sitting in front of me alive and kicking, but seems intent on insulting me.

'Deanna, stop being a bitch,' Danny says. 'The girl thought you were dead.'

'What have I done?' I eventually manage to say.

She doesn't answer me straight away. Instead she addresses Sebastian.

'Is my daughter more to your liking?' she asks.

'Clearly, since it's my ring she's wearing,' Sebastian bites back.

She then turns towards my godparents and eyes them up, stopping at Uz.

'Nice to see you again Uzrel. It seems you got a little promotion.'

'Well Williamina was never one to be really trusted,' Uz answered.

'She and I always had a understanding,' she responds.

'Well Micka soon put a stop to that,' Uz sneers.

Something changes in her face at his name and slowly moves her attention to where he stands. Her body is almost touching his, yet he remains stock still.

'Micka, my love,' she says silkly. 'I see you and my daughter have become closer than I'd wished.'

Then it hits me like a fast moving train and bile rises to my throat. I can see it, even feel it. The tension between my protector and mother. He is the angel that my mother fell in love with before my father. Like mother like daughter.

'Deanna, you can't blame Mina for your own failings,' he says.

My body tenses as she moves closer to him, her face is rigid with anger.

'Tell me Micka, what does she have that I never?'

'A pure heart.'

The slap she gives him resounds in the room and Sebastian grabs my arm to keep me still. But it's what she says next that sends me over the edge.

'I bet you told her you were pure too. An angel virgin who would only give yourself to her. Did you forget your moment of weakness and how sure I was that Mina was yours?'

Her laugh follows me up the stairs to the bathroom where I vomit into the toilet. The whole world is spinning and I'm in no position to stop it.

This is it. This is my limit. They've all pushed and pulled me and now it's gone too far. I feel someone enter the room and I know it's Micka. He sits on the floor and waits for me to finish.

'I can't do this anymore. I've no fight left,' I sob.

'You must know she's lying. She wants you to react and you're making it easy.'

'Are you the one she was in love with? The reason Sebastian walked away?'

'So I am told. When your grandfather was alive, he kept Deanna and Danny away from the angels, but once he died that was when we knew that Deanna existed. Of course the Powers were all over her like a rash and I was sent to watch her. She was this seventeen year old young woman who was fully aware of her power. She knew how important she was and that made her cocky. Every Marley trick she tried to pull to catch my attention didn't work. I wasn't built to love or feel anything. She became obsessed and when Sebastian arrived, she wouldn't accept him and we all left her.'

'And what about Ray?' I ask.

'Do you really want to know?'

I nod and he sighs as I sit down beside him, my head on his shoulder. Now I know he and my mother had not been together the urge to vomit has gone.

'The Powers knew that Deanna wasn't the fabled Marley woman they needed, but they knew it would have to be soon so they hedged their bets. The only way to get that woman was for it to be pure born, so they tried to enforce Deanna and Danny into creating a pure born girl.'

'Yes I know,' I say.

'Well Ray was already under Deanna's spell and he saved her from the Powers. That act broke through Deanna's walls and they fell in love. Nine months later you were born. She couldn't cope with knowing you would be Lilith incarnate and take her crown. She fooled us all, Ray most of all, of being the loving mother. Jealousy was always Deanna's downfall and when you were three years old that jealousy go the better of her. We had to banish her for your own safety.'

'And my father?'

'You know how much he loved your mother. He was blind to any reasoning. His mind was messed with. We faked a memory of her death.'

'How did you banish her and why is she here now?'

'Aslong as your Guardian Angel was in Supton you would be protected from her, but something has happened for her to break through now.'

'Michael?'

'Yes, maybe,' Micka sighs. 'He's been chipping away for so long our defences are weak.'

We sit in silence for a moment as I try and soak up all what he's told me. This mother that I'd always dreamt of has never really existed. This woman my father pined for never really existed. I have to accept that the woman who brought me into this world hates me more than she should. The reality is, I mourned her years ago. That woman in there now may have pushed me out of her body, but she is not my mother.

'So why am I so different to her?' I ask. 'Why do you love me so much?'

'You heard what I said. No matter what blood runs through your veins, you've the purest of hearts.'

Turning my face to his, I see all the love that Candice told me was there. He'd never stopped loving me. He was just trying to do the right thing. My next move surprises me, but I still do it. Leaning towards him, I place my lips on his and his breath catches, but doesn't stop. I've missed his warmth and the feel of his skin on mine and there's a real need for it now.

The kiss deepens as our passion starts to consume. Pulling his shirt open, he tugs mine free and we kiss and touch naked skin. It feels familiar and safe. Undoing his jeans, I struggle out of mine, before hovering over his lap.

'We shouldn't,' he whispers.

'Do you want me to stop?' I murmur against his mouth.

'This isn't the place, but I want you so much,' he replies.

Without any more words spoken we make love there on Sebastian's bathroom floor. It's passionate and frenzied, but also quiet. I've missed how his body feels against mine, in mine. How could I ever think that I could let him go?

'I know you have to marry him,' Micka says into my hair as we calm down after the climax.

'Having to doesn't mean I want to,' I answer.

Lifting my head so I look in his eyes, he smiles.

'I know. Stand strong that's all I ask. Stand strong. Now we must go downstairs once you've sorted yourself.'

By the time we both go down my mother has left and I try to hide any guilt that I may be feeling, but everyone seems too preoccupied to really notice that Micka and I have returned.

'Where has she gone?' I ask.

They all turn around and Sebastian grabs me into a hug. I try not to tense in his arms. I've washed, but I'm still aware of Micka's scent.

'I am so sorry that you had to find out that way. We just were trying to protect you,' he says.

'I need to talk to Danny alone please,' I ask.

Sebastian nods and grabs Danny.

'Take her upstairs to one of the other rooms.'

I lead him to into one of the spare rooms and close us in. I want him to tell me everything from his point of view.

Mother's Ruin

Danny's Journal 11th August 2230hrs

'Tell me everything. Marley to Marley.'

Mina stood there looking at me waiting for answers I didn't want to give. The pretence that my sister was dead was much easier to handle than this. Of course we'd hoped that Deanna would just go away quietly, but even I was doubtful, but she did. Pure silence until now. Mina is looking at me for answers and I've got to give it to her.

'What did Micka tell you?'

Her body flinches as I ask the question. I'm not stupid. Mina doesn't do hiding her guilt very well. But I don't really care about what she and Micka did while alone. She's her own woman.

'He told me that my mother, Deanna didn't want me?'

Tears start to fall down her cheeks. Shit! How can I do this to her? But she's asked so I tell her about the night her mother wanted to end Mina's life.

Mina had just turned three years old and Deanna had spent the past years coming to terms with the fact that her crown had been lost. Unbeknown to Ray, she had been trying to trace Sebastian. She wanted to negotiate a deal with him. She would leave Ray and be his wife, if he made her his queen. He refused to see her. It was Gabriel that stepped in. Told her that this wasn't something she could negotiate.

'You are not the Primum and never will be,' he told her.

'But I am the first Marley woman in a thousand years. I must be the Primum,' she argued.

'You're right, but the daughter you've borne has been born with her angel sister. She is the true Primum and there's nothing you can do to change that.'

'Just wait and see,' she said.

Deanna returned to Supton and we believed that she would accept Gabriel's word. Three days later, Deanna and Mina had disappeared. A note left saying that the Powers could go to hell. If she couldn't be the Primum than neither would Mina. She was prepared to destroy her daughter to make a point.

When found by Micka, he wanted to kill Deanna instantly. She had already gained support from the demons, and angel and demon fought each other on human soil for the first time since the Great Fall. Of course it wasn't nearly on the same scale. Humans just believed that it was a pocket of rioting. When Micka took Deanna the fighting ended, but Ray begged the angels to let her live, so she was banished and Ray's memories of a dead wife were created.

'Why was she so desperate to be the Primum?' Mina asks.

'Your grandfather had drilled it into her since she could understand that she was special. She would have the man of her dreams and be the greatest female that ever walked with the humans.'

'He sounds like an arsehole,' she says.

I can't argue with her on that. At least there's the start of a smile on that tear stained face of hers. It's not easy knowing that the person who is supposed to love and protect you is the enemy.

'It seems it's been Deanna that's been behind the whole Emandato. Michael has given her the power to destroy you.'

Mina's face pales further. She knows just as I do that the only way to end this is the death of another parent. The mother she's always missed and loved.

After leaving her in Sebastian's hands, I made my way back to the house. I should really start calling it home, but it's difficult. There's too much here for me to call it that.

Anyway, as I open the front door, there she waits, my beloved twin sister. The other half of my life. She is still beautiful. Age doesn't seem to have touched her. I wish I could say the same. But underneath all the love I have for her is the age old resentment. She was the wanted child and I was nothing more but a male stud to breed more Marleys.

'Is there no kiss for your sister?' she asks.

'Deanna, don't!'

She moves towards me, her body touching mine. She still knows how to use what she was born with, but I've lived with her long enough and I push her away. She tries the sulky pout that always used to work for everyone.

'That doesn't work on me,' I say.

'Fine, be like that,' she huffs. 'I get you're all pissy about the whole Emandato thing.'

'How could you? Mina is flesh and blood,' I snap.

Deanna shrugs as she circles the room. She stops at the fireplace where there's still pictures of Mina and Ray. She picks one up for a moment before placing it back.

'You came to the funeral?' I ask.

'Yes, he was my husband and despite what you all think I did love him.'

'You call that love? Trying to get in Sebastian's bed and then trying to destroy your daughter.'

Deanna snaps around and I feel the power of her temper.

'You have no idea what was going on. What I felt.'

'Deanna, you were and still are a selfish bitch.'

She doesn't answer and the tension is building between us. A silent Deanna is never a good thing. She's weighing things up. Trying to weigh up her options. We are both equals. Marley equals and she knows I have just as much power, but whereas she was always keen to show it, I wanted mine to disappear.

'So you live here now?' she asks, finally.

'Mina wanted me to have what was originally ours. If you bothered to get to know her, then you'd know she's a good girl.'

'You think I haven't kept tabs on my own daughter. I know what and who she is. But my agenda is still the same. She should never have been born. What she has should be mine.'

'Are we talking about Sebastian or Micka here?' I dare to ask.

Her face stiffens and I recognise the look. Mina has the same expression when dealing with Micka and Sebastian.

'I loved Micka first. He was mine,' she hisses.

'You gave him to her the day she was baptised.'

'That wasn't my idea,' she snaps.

Her face flushes. I've really hit a nerve there.

'It seems Ray wasn't as stupid as you believed.'

'No, he wasn't,' she mutters.

'So, when did Michael get involved?'

'I won't discuss him with you. He and I have an understanding.'

Obviously she's not going to tell me anything. She's not stupid and Michael is a strong angel to have on side.

'I heard a rumour that another Marley may be on its way,' she says.

This makes me uneasy. How much does Michael know so much about this town and my family? The problem is that there's no point in denying it either.

'So I believe, but don't worry it's not your turn to be called Grandmother this time. This is my family not yours.'

Deanna smiles and her eyes look past me and suddenly I feel incredibly cold. Slowly, I turn and there he is listening to every word just said.

'How are you going to be a grandfather?' he whispers.

'Jono, Gabriel just said that it was felt and it's not Mina's.'

'Well I've been careful, so it's not mine…unless.'

Then he's gone. Out the door leaving me and Deanna alone.

'Like father like son,' she sneers. 'Danny, I am going to get what I want and this town will accept me as their queen. You've just got to decide whether your loyalty is to me, your blood born sister or the half-breed that should never have been born.'

She then leaves without my answer. Emotional blackmail has always been her weapon of choice, but I'm not sure I can choose between them both. But right now, I need to try and find Jono and he won't answer the phone. I just hope he doesn't do something stupid

Phone Message from Jono to Jaq

'I know you're avoiding my calls. I've just heard some news that maybe of interest. Do you know anything about that?'

'Jaq, I swear if you don't pick up this phone I will come to the house and drag you out even if you're with Dom. I want answers.'

Jaq's Phone call to Carla 13th August 2230hrs

'Carla, I'm in the car right now coming over to you. Jono knows. I don't know how, but he knows and he wants answers. I can't face him.'

Mother's Ruin Pt2

Tannini's Journal 14th August 0230hrs

I have just returned from a well needed run and
fuck me I needed it. Seeing Deanna Marley in town
was a fucking punch in the stomach. I thought she
was dead. I went to her bleeding funeral. Watched
Ray put her in the ground. How the fuck is she in
Supton?

Deanna was a good woman and always seemed to
do a lot for those of us who lived here. Christ, she
helped me out and got me onto my feet. I loved her
like a sister, but this whole town loved her. They all
mourned her.

Now they all know they've been manipulated and
why. They will be split into who they love more,
Deanna or Mina. For me, the choice is easy. Mina is
like a daughter to me and knowing that Deanna
wanted her dead makes me sick. Was she really that
desperate to be with Sebastian?

Well there's no accounting for taste.

What I didn't know was the incident with Micka.
Man! That must sting. The mother can't catch the
attention of the one angel that her daughter catches
with no problem what so ever.

At least now I know that Deanna was the puppet
master to Williamina and Luca. Of course having
Michael on her shoulder would have helped. But it
leaves me to wonder why Michael is using her. She
is a Marley and Michael notoriously hates all
Marleys. They are the symbol of his father's
mistake. What has separated his brothers since
human time began. Lucifer, he could deal with, but

never Gabriel. That brother was untouchable. Too beloved.

Those at the Council have always revered Gabriel. Knowing that he was always would stand by all Others.

I remember Mina's baptism so very clearly. I was living with the Marleys then. It was just before my move to the city. The fights between Deanna and Ray were immense. The house shaking as her temper flew. The reason. Micka had been chosen to be Mina's protector. Of course I had no idea why then. I just figured it was Deanna's way of maintaining some control. She hated having the angels interfere with everything and she particularly hated Gabriel.

'Your daughter will be protected by the best angels we can offer. The Powers have demanded it so,' he said.

'She is not yours to use as you will. I forbid it,' Deanna argued.

But she didn't have a leg to stand on. What the Powers want they always get. Williamina the Guardian, Uzrel the Advisor, Cladiel the Heart and Micka the Protector. Each holding a stake in Mina's life.

'Promise me Ray on our wedding vows, never let Micka anywhere near her when she grows. They must never be in each other's life.' She begged.

'I swear, I will not let him near her when she grows,' Ray promised.

So they all stood there and made their vows to give themselves to this tiny redheaded baby, while its mother scowled on. A day of celebration, but with an undertone of tension. Now I think about it Micka didn't stay too long after the ceremony.

I have had no choice but to speak to the Council about Deanna's appearance. They too were shocked at how she'd remained hidden for so long. They have decided commune with all the other Other elder and royal houses.

'If Deanna is being governed by Michael then we all need to protect our Primum.'

I then contacted Sammy and just got her voicemail. That's when I decided on a run to clear my head.

Now while I write this, dawn is here and I'm exhausted. I've to be at the station in a few hours all my officers are going to be put on high alert. I best get some sleep.

Mina's Online Blog 16th August 2230hrs

I've been locked in the Manor for days and cabin fever is setting in. Mother dearest is working her way around town causing chaos. After the first few nights crying into my pillow wondering why my mother hated me, comes the reality that the woman holding the title of Deanna Marley is not my mother, because she's dead. This Deanna Marley is nothing but a chewed up old bitch. This woman turned my first guardian angel against me. Sent a Militant to mess with my head and then finish me. I have survived all of this and more. This I can beat too.

Sebastian has fussed over me as usual, but also been in constant contact with someone on the phone. My questions have been ignored. He's riled and tension is so high that I've resorted to sleeping in another room.

'Is there any more about my life that is a lie?' I asked.

'Mina, I don't have time for any more dramatics. We saved your life and did what we thought was best,' he snapped.

I hate us fighting, but we never seem to catch a break. But I suppose this is the test that we must pass. To prove to the Powers we are meant to be together. Although, I have no understanding of why. We apparently were made together as a perfect fit and yet it seems, we just rub each other in the wrong way.

This morning, however, I'd had enough of sleeping alone so crawling out of my bed, I made my way towards Sebastian's. Crawling under the covers, I snuggle into his warmth, but he doesn't respond to me. So I use some tactics to get his attention, but he's just lying there.

'What happened in the bathroom between you and Micka?'

I'm not prepared for the question, even though I should be.

'We just talked,' I lie.

Sebastian turns face me in bed and the neutral face I'm learning to have is there.

'I know you feel that everyone has lied to you, but I've always tried to be honest. When you've asked me, I have always given you the truth. Now I will ask you again. What happened between you and Micka in my bathroom?'

My heart is pounding because I hate lying, but if I fuck this up then Joe will make me pay.

'I've told you we talked. He told me about my mother and him and that's it. I told you when I came back that Micka was mistake.'

'But do you mean it Mina? I'm not blind, I see it. His eyes follow you around the room, yet you don't look at him.'

'And the problem is?'

'Why don't you look at him?'

'Because he means nothing.'

'Or he means too much that just by looking at him you're scared you will reveal yourself.'

'You are over thinking,' I say finally. 'I don't look at him, because I don't need to. He's not even there to me.'

'Yet you ran from the room…'

'For fucks sake, Sebastian. I ran from the room, because my mother suggested that the man I was once fucking could have been my father.'

He looks at me for a moment and then he pulls me into his arms.

'I'm sorry, I know this is been very stressful and I've not been at my most supportive,' he whispers.

'We will soon be married and then we can leave them to it,' I say.

He pushes my body into the bed with his own and I wrap my legs around his waist as he kisses down my neck to breasts. Pulling my night shirt free, he pinches my nipples and I squeal out in protest.

'Are you okay?' he asks.

'Yes, they are just tender, I must be premenstrual,' I say.

We make love, but it's uncomfortable. Everything feels like it's so sensitive. My body is on fire and not in the good way. I then do the very thing I've never had to do with him and fake my orgasm in order to get him to finish quickly. I've no idea if he knows. I just hope I convinced him.

After my shower, there was a voicemail from Carla, Jaq's older sister. She sounds frantic so I dial the number. All I hear is Jono and Jaq and without a word to Sebastian, I'm in the car heading for the city. I manage a text to Sebastian, who rings me.

'Why do you have to keep disappearing? You know the situation,' he snaps.

'I know, but this is my cousin and my best friend,' I answer.

The phone goes dead and I think I may have got away with it until a small breeze fills the car.

'Oh for fucks sake,' I hiss as Gabriel settles down beside me in the car. 'Did Sebastian send you?'

'I don't take orders from him. I came to watch over you. He does have a point. Your mother and my brother are after blood.'

'I know, but something has kicked off and all I know is that Jono is holding Jaq hostage and I've no idea why.'

'Would it help if I tell you why? Then maybe you'll stop driving like a mad woman,' he says.

'Fine, tell me.'

'We think Jaq is pregnant with Jono's baby.'

I slam hard on the breaks skidding to a halt. The car behind me honks its horn as it drives past. The driver flips me the finger, but I don't care. I'm still in shock at what Gabriel's just told me.

'Jaq is with Dom,' I say starting the engine and pulling off to the side.

'What can I say? A new generation of Marley is apparent and Jono's going after Jaq suggests that she is carrying his child.'

'Jaq will be scared,' I say. 'I think I know what she's going to do.'

'Then you best get us to the city safely.'

As I drive I try and get my head around what Gabriel has just told me. How could I not know? but when I think about it. The weight she's put on. The glow in her face. But I've been so preoccupied I've not seen. As far as I was concerned she and Dom were solid, but then why am I surprised. Jaq and Jono have always had something. That spark that has burned ever since we were kids must have really blown into a full blame flame. But how could they be so stupid and not take precautions. The thought of anther line of Marleys going through what we have is unthinkable.

'Is it a girl?' I ask finally.

Gabriel glances my way.

'Why do you ask?'

'It's just a question,' I answer.

'You think that if it's a girl, then we can leave you to be with Micka and we can offer this child to Sebastian as the next best thing?'

'That's not...'

'Mina, we don't just hand Marley girls over. Your mother was not chosen, because she wasn't you. You are the Primum. You are Lilith and YOU belong to Sebastian. Plus, ask yourself would you let your niece go through what you have, just so you can have your angel?'

'No,' I mutter. 'I didn't think.'

Now guilt is rippling through me, because that damn angel read every instinct of mine and more.

'Anyway it's not for me to know and plus you and your mother were a rarity. It's probably a boy.'

For the rest of the journey, I'm lost in my thoughts and ignore Gabriel, who seems content to listen to the radio. Every now and then changing channel before humming to the tune. Finally, I get to where Jaq's sister waits.

It has been a while since I've seen her and she's not changed much. Still beautiful in an understated way. Worry covers her face as she rushes to embrace me.

'Tell me,' I say.

She says that Jono arrived at her apartment demanding to see Jaq. An argument had brewed between them and they both had driven off. The last message Jaq had sent was that Jono was refusing to let her leave the car.

'Gabriel, can you take me to them?'

With a nod, we are there in some car park where I can hear them both screaming at each other. Jono's power is peaking, because I can feel it, but I need to go in.

'Wait here,' I say to Gabriel and to my surprise there's no argument.

Walking to the car, I bang on the window and both of them silence.

'Open the fucking door now,' I snap.

They both look at me and the back door pops its lock. Climbing in I have to take a breath because the power in such a small place is suffocating.

'What the fuck are you both playing at?'

'This selfish bitch never told me about our child and I think she wants to kill it,' Jono hisses.

'And told your fuckhead of a cousin, that this is none of his business. It's my body and I will do what I like,' Jaq shouts back.

'Right first of all, Jono turn down your mojo I can barely breathe in here and secondly, Jaq if you're having Jono's baby then it is his business.'

'It's not Jono's it's Doms, that's what I'm trying to tell you,' she says.

'Jono get out of the car,' I say.

'No fucking way, I'm staying.'

'Jono get out the fucking car now.'

He gives a poisonous look and cussing, slams the door as he storms out and stands with Gabriel.

'Right, now pighead has gone, tell me the truth.'

Tears roll down Jaq's eyes and rummaging around the glove compartment, I find her a tissue. She sniffs into it and then takes a deep breath.

'I thought it was Jono's. That's the truth and I was scared. I didn't want to bring another Marley into the world just to have it go through the shit you and he have. So Carla suggested that I come to the city and she could help me find out the father.'

'And did you?'

She nods. 'There's a guy who can tell what the breed of a child is if they're a mixbreed Other. So I went to him and he's in no doubt that my baby is half Fae and half Necromancer.'

'You're sure?' I ask.

'Yes, without a doubt. This child isn't Jono's and I'm betting half the town will know by now which means I have to explain things to Dom,' she says through her tears.

'Only I know. It was Gabriel that told me. Look don't worry about anything. Just go back to Carla's and have a few days. Leave Jono to me.'

I give her a hug and then leave her to drive off.

'Why the fuck did you let her leave?' Jono raves.

With a swift movement I slap him across the face causing him to stumble back.

'Get a grip you stupid arse.' Then turning to Gabriel. 'Your sources are wrong, that baby is not a Marley, it's half necromancer.'

'She's lying,' Jono says.

'She's been tested, she knows who the father is and you need to apologise.'

'Maybe,' Gabriel says. 'But it's rarely wrong. Another Marley has been created.'

An uneasy silence descends on the group. Then suddenly something hits me in the stomach with such a force that I nearly vomit. Gabriel catches me eye and he must see my fear. The mental calculation that I'm hurriedly doing in my head.

'Mina,' he says as I take a step back. 'Don't bolt.'

Taking another step back, I feel I can't breathe.

'Oh shit!' Jono says. 'It's you.'

'No, it can't be,' I whisper.

Before I can say another word Gabriel has zapped us back to my flat at Mina's and in his hands he holds the test kit.

'I don't want to,' I say.

'Mina, we need to be sure. I thought it was you at first, but then there's been nothing. Either you are carrying the next generation or our sources are wrong and we need to look into that.'

'Your sources are wrong,' I argue.

'Take the test or I will go deeper and will find out myself and believe me that will hurt.'

Snatching the test from his hand, I shut myself in the bathroom. The thought that I may be pregnant disturbs me. There's no way I want to bring another Marley into this world. Not only that, but judging by that last time I bled, can I even be sure that the child is Sebastian's. I know Micka didn't fall, but something deep inside tells me that it could be Micka's.

I look down at the used wand in my hand and lower myself onto the floor. Two blue lines. The test is positive and now I realise what happened on the Day of the Dragon. That was the day I conceived. The day I peaked and the day I slept with the two men in my life. Now I know that I'm with child, there's an impossible choice. I'm already lying to Sebastian, but Joe's threat means I may have to serve my biggest lie yet. Tell him that he and I will be parents, no matter who the true father is.

8225256R00136

Printed in Great Britain
by Amazon.co.uk, Ltd.,
Marston Gate.